Praise for *The Caprices:*

"Murray writes stories of fierce intensity, stories that are evocative, distinct, and haunting. . . . Dark and unflinching, these brimming, sometimes jagged stories endure powerfully in the reader's memory as they reach across continents and time with precision and—in the heart of darkness—a measure of grace."
—Claire Messud, *The New York Times Book Review*

"War is an unusual subject for a young female writer; with each piece, Murray proves to be increasingly exceptional."
—*Publishers Weekly* (starred review)

"[*The Caprices*] is a wrenching account of war taken personally."
—Barbara Lloyd McMichael, *The Seattle Times*

"There is no denying that [*The Caprices*] is indeed an artistic achievement."   —Terry Hong, *The Bloomsbury Review*

"In this sobering book, [Murray] turns the bombed-out and broken setting of World War II into a theater for humankind, where both weakness and grace are writ large."
—*The Washington Post*

"A feverish combination of passion and lucidity."
—Valerie Martin, author of *Property* and *Mary Reilly*

"Along with these characters—inside their skins, their very bones—we learn, sometimes unwillingly, more of the possibilities that arise with being human."
—Kate Wheeler, author of *When Mountains Walked*

THE
CAPRICES

Sabina Murray

GROVE PRESS
New York

Originally published by in the United States in 2002 by Mariner Books,
a division of Houghton Mifflin Company

Published simultaneously in Canada
Printed in the United States of America

Library of Congress Cataloging-in-Publication Data
Murray, Sabina.
The caprices / Sabina Murray.
p. cm.
ISBN-10: 0-8021-4313-X
ISBN-13: 978-0-8021-4313-6
1. World War, 1939–1945—Campaigns—Pacific Area—Fiction.
2. Pacific Area—Fiction.   3. War stories, American.   I. Title.
PS3563.U787 C36 2001
813'.54—dc21   2001024527

Some of the stories in this collection have appeared elsewhere in slightly different form:
"Intramuros" in *Ploughshares,* "The Caprices" in *New England Review,* "Walkabout" in
Ontario Review, "Folly" in *Charlie Chan Is Dead 2: At Home in the World,* edited by
Jessica Hagedom, and "Position" in *The Norton Anthology of Short Fiction, 7th Edition.*

Grove Press
an imprint of Grove/Atlantic, Inc.
841 Broadway
New York, NY 10003

Distributed by Publishers Group West

www.groveatlantic.com

07 08 09 10 11 12   10 9 8 7 6 5 4 3 2 1

For my mother

Acknowledgments

I would like to thank Don Hymans, Heidi Pitlor, Valerie Martin, and the Bunting Fellowship Program at the Radcliffe Institute of Harvard University.

I am grateful to my husband, John, and son, Nicholas, and to the rest of my family, without whom I would not have been able to write this book.

Contents

The Caprices

.

Tʜɪs ᴄᴏᴜʟᴅ ʙᴇ any village street. The packed dirt could cover any country road, and the dust that rises in billowing sheets, lifted by the lazy hands of the dry season, could menace any provincial town. It is three o'clock in the afternoon, but no children wander back from school. The Chinese shopkeeper's door has been shut for nearly a year, but no matter, since the children will not bother him for moon cakes, sweet wafers, and candied tamarind. A kalesa driver sits idly by his cart; his horse, unperturbed by the state of affairs, dozes behind blinkers, flicking rhythmically with his tail, one rear hoof casually cocked to bear no weight. In response to a fly, the horse shakes his head, jangling gear and whipping his mane from side to side. The fly rises up, buzzing at a higher pitch.

What you are witnessing is war.

A woman in a faded floral shift slowly makes her way down the sidewalk. She carries two huge woven bags; one is full of vegetables, the other holds a few canned goods and some dried fish, although a year ago this bag would have been full of meat. The woman has black hair, which she has pulled into a tight bun. Even streaks of gray (a new appearance this last year) break through the black. Her face is thin. She clenches her teeth with the effort necessary to carry her load. She sets down her bags, takes a deep breath, then manages a few more steps. The faded cloth of her dress is damp with perspiration. She wears a scarf wrapped around her neck, which must be uncomfortable in this heat. She sees the kalesa. She waves, then calls. The driver lifts his head. He was dreaming. The beautiful washerwoman was offering him a rice cake. The cake was blue. She was smiling at him with perfect teeth. "This is for you," she said. The beautiful washerwoman moved her hips from side to side. She smiled slyly. "Take the cake . . ."

And then the sight of Mrs. Garcia waving at him down the street. She can barely manage.

It is 1943.

Imagine, a woman of such standing carrying her own groceries, there on the street, bareheaded in the early afternoon heat. Imagine all that gray hair, overnight, it seems. He closes his eyes again; sadly, the beautiful washerwoman is gone. He pulls himself to his feet.

"*Oo po*," he shouts, although lazily, in Mrs. Garcia's direction. *Oo po*—the polite greeting, but the driver manages to make it sound like an insult. What will she do, this woman? She isn't wealthy anymore. She is merely someone who was once wealthy, which is still worth something—she has held on to her house. He pats his horse's dusty shoulder. What sentimental urge has made him keep Diablo alive? He knows the horse will be stew meat within a month or so. How can he feel sorry for his horse when his brother and little son are dead? It is easy to feel sorry for a horse, even easy to feel sorry for Mrs. Garcia, who has never had to carry bags before.

Trinidad watches her grandmother paying the kalesa driver. Auring, the maid, is standing at the gate. She tries to carry one of the bags, but can't even get it off the ground. Auring is very old

although she does not know her age. She remembers the great ty-
phoon of 1852. She tells Trinidad about it—the carabao lifted off
the ground as if God himself had reached down and carried it
off, how Mr. Pedrino's great-grandfather was decapitated by a
piece of flying tin while chasing his hat. Auring was Mrs. Garcia's
nanny, which is all well and good, but she is not much use as a
maid. Trinidad jumps off the window ledge. She runs down the
broad mahogany stairs.

"*Ija,* don't run," her grandmother says, but her voice is run-
down, and Trinidad can sense that she really doesn't care. "Call
Jose."

But Jose is standing in the doorway. He walks in the awkward,
dragging motion dictated by his clubfoot. He hooks his arm
through the handles of one bag, then grabs the other with his
good hand. Trinidad stares, as she has been told not to. Just a
forefinger and a thumb like a little bird's beak on his bad hand.
Jose can't even make them touch, these two pathetic digits. He
wiggles them toward each other constantly. Trinidad wonders
what would happen if they did touch, what magic this would
cause.

"Trinidad," her grandmother warns her, and Trinidad looks
down at the toes of her shoes. She begins edging backward up the
stairway. "Trinidad, what are you doing?"

"I am praying," she lies. "I am praying that God will see how
good I have become, and return Nanay and Tatay. I am praying
that the Japanese will go back to Japan." And Trinidad will go
back to Manila. She will walk between her parents on Saturday
afternoons as they make their way to the cinema to watch an
American movie. Vivien Leigh. Gary Cooper. Trinidad tells herself this, even though she knows her parents are dead. Now,
Trinidad can only go to mass with her grandmother and the ancient maid. She walks in the middle and Auring leans on her.
When Auring does this, Trinidad surreptitiously pinches her
arm. And Auring never complains. Close to a century of servi-

tude has taught her that much. They go to Santo Tomas with its paint-chipped idols—Santa Teresa, San Jose. Trinidad is a city girl. She does not want to die in this dusty provincial town. She does not even want to turn twelve here, and her birthday is only two months away.

Manila is dead.

Yesterday, Thursday, Trinidad found that her doll had suffered a haircut. She brought the doll to her grandmother. "Jose did it."

"How can you prove it, *ija?*"

"Who else?"

Mrs. Garcia knows that her granddaughter is right, but she is frightened of Jose—his deformity would scare anyone. She is also grateful to him. The Japanese have looted all the other large houses in the town. When they came to claim her house, they saw Jose dragging himself across the parquet floor with his head cradled in the crook of his shoulder—that hook of a hand pulling him along through the air, as if it anchored and reanchored him to an invisible weight. He frightened the Japanese. Who knows what they squawked at each other? But she knew. They saw the house and they wanted it; they saw Jose and they didn't. The Japanese thought the very walls were diseased.

Sergeant Shori checks that the lock on his bedroom door is secure, then unbuttons his jacket and carefully hangs it up in preparation for a siesta. Sergeant Shori is not accustomed to having so many people hate him. He is a schoolteacher. He has slender white hands that are good at painting, good at playing the piano. Now they carry a gun. He likes modern women with short hair. He likes opera, except for Puccini, who he feels is overrated. He likes European food. He hates the Philippines and often wonders why the emperor doesn't let these frightening aborigines have it back. Twice he has contracted malaria. Twice he has been sniped at and nearly killed, once when he was reliev-

ing himself in a banana grove. Shori is scared that the other officers will find out that he is weak, although he has no problem
with his actual weakness. To keep them from suspecting, Shori
says things that are particularly cruel. He has said, "I would like
the hand of a Filipino to take back to my father as a souvenir," although the thought of this disgusts him. He says, with feigned
enthusiasm, "I would gladly die for the emperor," instead of the
usual "I would die for the emperor," not realizing that the
"gladly" is what gives him away. Shori is a frightened man. He
feels his countrymen have gone mad in this land of rot and
horror. He only speaks to deceive them with his false loyalty. Se-
cretly, he feels that he has been transferred from Manila because
he does not get along with the other men. His is a solitary post.

The ring is heavy platinum set with a pale blue emerald-cut
diamond. He wears it on his left ring finger. The ring is rightfully
his. He was the officer in charge of possessing the house. He took
the ring, looted by Corporal Miwa, back in Intramuros last year;
yes, it is true that Shori waited outside. The killing of civilians is
distasteful to him, especially in the city, where one finds elegant
paneling in the living rooms, German crystal in the cabinets,
grand pianos that are perfectly tuned . . . No, he could not go
inside. This was the house of a lawyer with pro-American senti-
ments, Spanish ancestry, and most likely a radio. The locals
looked up to him.

Shori remembers taking the ring from Miwa. There was
blood on the band which had just started to dry and flake. Miwa
said that the ring had been on the lawyer's pinkie finger. It was
stuck. Miwa had cut the lawyer's finger off. A girl had cried out.
She must have been the man's daughter. She was gone, swallowed
in the mayhem. Miwa had killed two people in that house—first
the lawyer, then his wife. Miwa laughed when he remembered
the woman running at him with her fists.

Shori looks at the ring. Inside is an inscription. He can read
the letters, but he does not know what they mean. He does not

even know that the words are in Latin: *Semper Fidelis*. He can only point out *S* and *F*. Shori is a schoolteacher, not a scholar.

Trinidad throws her doll down at Jose, who is picking over a tray of rice.

"In Manila, we would have drowned you right after birth. We would have slid you out of your mother and straight into a bucket of soapy water. Slip."

Jose smiles at her. He is handsome with fine regular features and soft, straight hair. His eyes are lighter than most, more amber than brown. Jose has the face of an angel, they say, and the body of the devil himself. What a curse. Better to be ugly and understand your lot. Better to be miserable than dissatisfied. "Aren't you too old for dolls?"

Trinidad grabs back her doll. "Aren't you too mouthy for a halfwit, *deformado* servant?"

Jose laughs. In a way, he likes Trinidad, who takes herself so seriously. "Go away, little girl. I have to cook."

"Now?" It's only five and Trinidad wants to harass him. Jose cooks this meal every day at the same time. Trinidad has figured it out, but still the others persist in pretending she does not know.

Before the Japanese invaded, Trinidad and her brother spent long hours together. Their parents had forbidden them to leave the house. On this particular day, Miguel, who hardly ever bothered to speak to Trinidad, was telling stories. He laughed at Trinidad when she said that she couldn't wait to leave Manila. Why weren't they in the province, where it was safe?

"Safe? You think the house in the province is safe?"

"But Miguel, the Japanese are cannibals."

"Just listen." Miguel grew serious, which was a novelty. "About four years ago we were all in the province for the feast of San Isidro. I was running around with Jose. Anyway, he tells me that all the desserts for the big dinner are in the basement. He says they're hiding them there. But I know that they keep the basement locked. Even the stairs to the basement are always locked. But Jose knows where the key is. So he gives me this candle, and tells me to knock myself out."

Trinidad urged her brother to continue.

"I'm pretty excited. Jose lets me in at the top of the stairs. I go down to the basement. The key's hanging by the door and I have my candle. There's this huge padlock on the door, kind of a little grate section at the top, like a prison. So I put the key in the padlock." Miguel shuddered, then smiled broadly. "I'd rather deal with the Japanese."

"What happened?"

"So I'm down there, looking around in the dark, with my little candle, and that's just lighting up my stupid hand and nothing else, and it sure as hell doesn't smell like cake down there. It smells like a sewer, and I can hear water trickling, because I guess the creek runs by there, and I'm getting scared, because, as you know, I'm terrified of rats."

"Rats?"

"No, Trinidad, this is not a rat story."

"Cakes?"

"There sure as hell wasn't any cake down there." Miguel began to roll a cigarette, and Trinidad noticed that his hands were shaking. "Jesus, Mary, and Joseph . . ." he said to himself.

"So you're in Grandmama's basement . . ."

"They started yelling and screaming upstairs. I could hear them, Tatay in particular. They were yelling for me. And I'm thinking, It's just cake, and Tatay's yelling, 'Miguel, get out of there. Get out of there,' and I think I'm going to get the beating of my life, so I blow out the candle. I say to myself, 'I'll just sneak out, then say I was somewhere else.' So it's completely dark and I'm edging my way to the door, and they're all running around upstairs, boom boom boom, and down the stairs, boom boom boom, and I can see Tatay's silhouette on the wall because he's holding a candle. Now he's whispering my name, 'Miguel, please come out. Come out slowly and quietly.' And I'm thinking, When did he get so smart? But I'm smarter. So I stay hiding there, then I hear this shuffling near me and I think, Jesus, that has to be the biggest rat in the world, because it sounds like a person, then I think, That's no rat, that's a ghost, so I start screaming, and Tatay rushes in and grabs me . . ."

"And?"

"It wasn't a cake and it wasn't a rat." Miguel shook his head. "And it wasn't a ghost."

Shortly after Miguel told Trinidad that story, he disappeared. He sneaked out a window — said he needed a chocolate bar — and never came back. Sometimes Trinidad thinks he joined the guerrillas. He was fourteen, which isn't that young. Sometimes she knows better. She knows the Japanese and what they can do.

Jose puts on a clean T-shirt. He combs his hair, watching his distorted reflection. The tin back of the mirror is rotting. He is accompanying Mrs. Garcia on the bus today. Jose makes her feel safe. Jose is not scared of the Japanese. He is only scared of pain. "They torture," the other villagers say. "They rip off your fingernails. They fill your belly with water, then jump on you." These Japanese are an imaginative bunch. When Jose thinks of the pain they might inflict, the hair rises on the back of his neck. His lower back feels cold, wet chills. He fears the pain. He cannot associate it with the Japanese, like the others. He does not imagine Shori's face hanging golden in the sky as he faints away. But only the sensations of pain. How could the other villagers know what it is like? Were they born with the blueprint of self-torture in their genes? Do their bones rebel against them, twisting and pulling in the night, trying to flex themselves and correct their knotted bodies? When they go to sleep, do they fear waking to a nightmare cramp that strangles from the neck to the ankles? In a year or two, they will wake from the nightmare of war, and he, Jose, will only be delivered into another.

At first, Trinidad thought it was another of Miguel's elaborate lies. She lived in the big house with her grandmother, Jose, and Auring and feared nothing but the Japanese. She had no cause to go to the basement, but as the weeks passed certain oddities began to demand her attention. Although Trinidad had no business down there, it seemed that Jose, her grandmother, and Auring did; Auring went down at eleven A.M. and in the afternoon around five. Jose and her grandmother were not so regular, but many times Trinidad had caught her grandmother sighing heavily as she ascended the stairs, and once she had seen Jose, bucket in hand, at the top of the landing eyeing her guiltily. One night, when Trinidad had awoken as the result of a bad dream, she heard a distant moaning coming from somewhere in the house. In her dream, Miguel had appeared to her without hands. She asked him where they were.

"A Japanese officer cut them off," he said. "He sent them back to Japan for a souvenir."

Trinidad was eased to hear her grandmother's comforting footsteps on the stairs. She stumbled out to the landing in her bare feet.

"*Ija,* why are you up?"

"I had a bad dream. The Japanese will kill us."

"There is a good chance that will happen. The best thing you can do is go back to bed and pray for us. Pray for our souls."

"Even Jose's?"

"Especially Jose's. He really needs it."

Trinidad went back to bed. She did not pray. She listened to that faint moaning, which was answered by her grandmother's sweet whispers. Sometimes, when the wind was still, Trinidad could make out a few words. Once she heard her grandmother say, "I know you are lonely." And once, "You could kill us all."

But when the wind picked up, Trinidad was not sure if she had merely imagined those things.

One morning Trinidad followed Auring, who was carrying a bundle of rice and chicken wrapped in banana leaves, down the musty stairs. The air was moldy, damp and thick, but through this dull odor cut the acrid scent of urine—not cat piss, or rats; the smell was a distinctly human one. There was the door with the grating, as Miguel had said. There was the key on the nail. Auring, whispering softly, held the package up to the grating. Trinidad did not breathe. She watched in silence. A slender, white hand reached through the darkness, like a pale shoot pushing through soil. The nails were long and yellow. The hand took the small green package and slipped back into the mystery behind the door.

"Auring, who is that?"

Auring turned quickly, her hand held tight to her heart. "You will kill me," she said.

"Who is that?"

"Your grandmother will be angry."

"Only if I tell her."

It is a sad story. This woman in the basement is Trinidad's aunt. She killed a man, slit his throat with a kitchen knife. Mrs. Garcia hid her in the basement. She told the police that her daughter had escaped. This was in 1930. Since then, she has not left the basement.

The woman is mad.

Auring unwrapped the white handkerchief that was on her wrist for a bandage. There was a dark brown stain on the inside of the cloth. This was Auring's blood. Trinidad remembered the suspicious scarf that her grandmother had started wearing.

"She scratched me," Auring said.

Trinidad looked at the scratch. It was deep with ragged edges.

The scab had dried in yellow, crystal-like crusts. Auring's skin was thin, like onionskin Bible paper. Her veins were blue and prominent. Liver spots covered her arms in purples and pinks.

"Aren't you scared to feed her?"

"What is a scratch?" Auring said. "One day she will escape and kill us all, if the Japanese don't get us first."

"What is her name?"

Auring seemed surprised at the question. Perhaps because it was so predictable.

"Her name is Trinidad."

Shori thinks this village is hell on earth. It is only ten miles from Cabanatuan, the POW camp for American soldiers, which makes the natives surly. They know what goes on in the camp, and this constant proximity to cruelty and death has made them callous. He has the worst servants in the world. Their Japanese is terrible, and Shori, unlike some other officers, has learned no Tagalog. They are impervious to threats. Occasionally, he remembers that in Japan he had no servants and wasn't much more than a civil servant himself. Last time this thought entered his head, he beat the maid about her head with a shoe. She did not seem to care. She thought he was going to kill her. When he didn't, she looked down on him. But he did not kill her then. He would not do that for her, because her thoughts were of no consequence. Today he would beat her, because that was his whim. Tomorrow, he might decapitate her. He stands on the small balcony that extends out from his bedroom and looks over the street. He cannot sleep in this infernal heat. Some officers have the servants fan them during their nap, but Shori knows this is asking for a bolo in the gullet. He watches his maid go through the gate. What can she be up to? Shori yells to her.

She bows her head there in the street. She does this reflexively, so that she is bowing to no one, just bowing to the road in the direction of the town square. A thin, dirty dog hobbles by.

"Where are you going?" shouts Shori.

"To my sister's, sir," she says, addressing the dirt.

Shori remembers that he has given her permission to do this.

"You must tell me everything that is said."

Shori realizes what he has ordered. Will she tell him of whatever it is that women discuss? Will she tell him about babies? About dresses? About shampoo?

"I know that your sister is a guerrilla sympathizer!" he shouts after her.

The maid bows in the street again. She thinks that her fate and the fate of the whole village rest in the hands of this halfwit. Shori glares at her. How dare she think such thoughts. Luckily, he is too important to mind what she is thinking.

Trinidad will have to work efficiently. She does not even know what kind of man this Shori is, or what exactly she will say to him. She wonders if what the American said—if every Filipino killed one Japanese, the war would be over—is true, since he was hallucinating and half dead anyway. And he didn't kill any Japanese, but he sure as hell killed a whole houseful of Filipinos. All those Orosas dead. She remembered when the Japanese found out. They dragged the American into the street. The neighbors looked at each other's faces—the eyes—to see who the collaborator was. That was the first time Trinidad saw Shori. That was the first time she saw the ring.

The American begged Shori to let the Orosas go. He was so skinny, so close to the grave, it didn't seem worth killing him. The children had been joking about the American all week. "How did he get through the fence at Cabanatuan? He walked." Which was some local variation on the old "He's so skinny that when it's raining, he doesn't even get wet." They explained away the fact that he hadn't been shot with the same clever joke.

It wasn't Shori's sword that lopped off the American's head.

And Shori didn't kill the Orosas, although he did order that they be taken away—all of them, even the baby. But Shori is in charge in this small town. Every man, woman, and child bows to him. Every horse, house, and field belongs to him. Every dog shits because Shori has wished it, every fly buzzes because Shori allows it. Trinidad knows all of this, just as she knows that today the house will be empty. But she needs to be patient.

So much of war is waiting.

This afternoon Mrs. Garcia is taking the bus with Jose to the neighboring town to visit her cousin Lourdes. She does this every Friday. Now that she has Trinidad to care for, keeping up the Friday trip gets harder and harder. But she is the only one who visits the old woman. Imagine. She herself an old woman, visiting another. All the men are gone. She's lucky to have Jose around. He too would leave, crawl into the mountains, become a guerrilla, but he is too deformed to be of much use, even though he is clever. Jose is looking out the window. A group of Japanese soldiers are wading through a rice paddy, rifles ready. They flash by so quickly that Mrs. Garcia isn't even sure she saw them.

"Did you see that?" asks Jose.

"Don't let them see you looking." She says this more as a constant reminder than in response to current danger.

"An American must have escaped."

Mrs. Garcia did not want to leave Trinidad. She's worried about the child, but this is the same reason she doesn't want her on the bus. Who knows what she might say and who might hear it? When Trinidad first came to the province, she wouldn't speak. Now she speaks all the time, crazy stuff. What do you expect? Intramuros had been emptied of everyone she knew, and there she was—little Trinidad, wandering around. No one knows where her parents are, or Miguel, or what happened to the house. Mrs. Garcia pushes a tear off her cheek with the back of her hand. She grimaces when she does this, as though dust has irritated her eyes. Yes, her stupid son probably was keeping a radio. All those years of law school down the drain.

Shori hears banging on the metal gate. Will he never be able to take his nap? He peeks out of the door. He hears his houseboy's voice. "Important that sir sleep." But curiosity gets the better of him and he steps onto his balcony. There are two soldiers.

"What brings you here?" asks Shori.

"An American has escaped."

"Have you alerted the guard?" "Woken up" would be better. That fat ass sits in the pillbox all day. He should drink. That would be better than this nameless, compulsive sloth. Sleep. Sleep. Sleep. Shori has told the guard to keep the natives on their toes. The guard has interpreted this creatively. Shori has seen a woman creep into the pillbox. He has seen her creep out, her hands bulging with cigarettes. He wanted to say something, but was worried. That guard knows that Shori spends all day in his house. He probably senses that Shori just wants the war to be over, that he is thinking, If the Americans invade, I can go home. Shori must pluck out this ugly thought time and time again, as if it were a stubborn weed. Better not to stir the guard. Better to leave him sedated with food and aboriginal sex. How sympathetic everyone would be if they only knew how hard it is to govern.

Trinidad pushes open the gate. She looks up and down the street. No one is about, except for a lame dog hobbling along. He stops to sniff at some garbage. Trinidad wonders why no one has eaten him yet. She slips through the gate, pulling it shut behind her. She is wearing her good patent leather shoes with the shiny buckles. Some sense of occasion has made her do this. She has plaited her hair; the right braid is perfect, but the left has ridged bumps rising out from the part. No matter. She has more important things to think about. The woman in the basement is angry;

her moaning kept Trinidad up all night. But Trinidad's mind is still clear. She walks quickly, not looking to the right or left. She would like to get there before people start waking up from their siestas.

Mrs. Garcia massages her cousin's legs. High blood pressure. Poor Lourdes. And she no longer has her medicine.

"How does that feel?"

"Good, of course," says Lourdes.

"This war is bad for all of us."

Lourdes laughs, sticking her tongue through the gap where her two front teeth once stood guard. She laughs, poking her tongue through this space, making a hissing sound. "War or no war, I am supposed to die. I am an old woman with a bad heart. No injustice there."

Mrs. Garcia's eyes fill with tears, but she catches herself just in time. Her eyes are wells, but no tears fall.

"What are you thinking of?" Lourdes asks.

"Even without this war, you will die. I have no hope of keeping you around. I have already started to miss you." Mrs. Garcia leans back to sit on the floor. She gives up her stoicism and lets the tears roll down her face.

Lourdes starts to laugh again, in sympathy for her cousin. "At least I won't have to live much longer under the Japanese." She leans back in her rocker. "And to think, you're just waiting for the Americans to return."

Mrs. Garcia looks at her cousin. She is right.

"Why is it," says Lourdes, "that every damned time one conqueror shoots at another, there's some stupid Filipino standing in the middle?"

Lourdes plants her crooked forefinger in the center of her forehead.

This, finally, makes Mrs. Garcia laugh.

· · ·

How can there be another person at the gate? And this time, Shori really was about to drift off. Dreams are the only escape from this place. Shori can hear the houseboy. It's Tagalog. What business can a native have at his doorstep? Shori pulls himself up. He walks again to the balcony. Walking is like swimming in this heat. There is a girl at the gate.

"Are you selling something?" asks Shori.

The girl immediately bows her head. She is silent.

"What does she want?"

"I don't know, sir," says the houseboy. "She insists on seeing you. She says it is important."

"What do you want?" Shori asks.

"American." Trinidad is unaware of the lucky coincidence that day. Shori waves her inside. He was hoping that the American would surface in some other town. Who knows? Maybe this girl is lying.

Jose is almost finished with the living room floor. Mrs. Aragon says that she is nearly blind and doesn't care about the state of the floors anymore. But Mrs. Garcia insists. Every Friday Jose sets to working the red wax into the floorboards, polishing with the coconut husk beneath his foot. This takes him longer than most, but who else will do it? It is hot, but Mrs. Garcia is wearing a scarf. Earlier, when she thought Jose was not looking, she unwrapped it for Mrs. Aragon to see the deep scratches in her neck —five neatly spaced lines as though intended for music. And imagine. That little *loca* Trinidad asking him that morning what was up with the scarf. Why would her grandmother wear such a thing in this heat? Maybe she wasn't faking. Maybe Trinidad really can't remember. Jose picks a sliver of red wax from beneath his thumbnail. That would really be frightening, if she couldn't remember.

· · ·

Who would have known that in addition to the usual ills of the Japanese, this man was a pervert? It is Friday, and everyone knows that Mrs. Garcia takes the bus to visit her cousin Mrs. Aragon, that she takes Jose along with her, that the stately—although run-down—house, shaded by tamarind trees and hidden behind an imposing wall, is empty except for Trinidad. He does not know if he wants to be a part of this, even if he is just driving them there. He is just the kalesa driver, not the moral police. Diablo clops along at a steady rate with his head, as always, leaning to the left. It makes you think you're headed in that direction, but no; Diablo's head goes to the left, but his hoofs go straight. I am just a kalesa driver, he reminds himself. Then he sneaks a peek, pretending to check the sky for an improbable rain cloud. He processes his mental picture at leisure. Shori seems harassed. His hair is uncombed, which is unusual for him. The top button of his jacket is undone. Trinidad looks straight ahead. She is wearing her Sunday clothes. She seems very determined. What a serious little girl this Trinidad is. He wonders if what they say about her is true. Is she really demented? She must be. Why else would she be taking Shori to her house? But wait.

"Americano?" asks Shori, doubting and threatening at the same time. He pulls at the collar of his shirt.

"Americano," replies Trinidad with a solemn nod.

Is there an escaped American in the Garcia house?

Trinidad sees the ring glinting on Shori's finger. This has been much easier than she imagined. She did not know that an American had escaped from the camp. She was going to tell Shori's houseboy that the American was a guerrilla sneaking out of the mountains, that he was injured and needed a place to stay for a few days. The houseboy could relay anything you needed to communicate to Shori, but Shori had come without any explaining on her part.

Shori notices her eyeing the ring. He flexes his fingers in an effeminate way. This reminds Trinidad of a stretching cat. There is much of a cat about this man. His whiskers sprout strangely from the sides of his face. His nose is small, upturned. His upper lip is soft and fleshy, plumping over the lower, and when he speaks she sees the tips of two triangular incisors extending down from the row of yellowed teeth. Not like a man at all, really. This morning Trinidad instructed Auring to leave the doorway to the basement stairs unlocked. Auring looked suspicious. No, more worried, but Auring will say nothing. Trinidad knows this with great certainty, although she is not sure why.

Mrs. Garcia is cutting slices of bibingka for herself and for her cousin. Then she remembers Jose and cuts a piece for him, since it is his favorite sweet. Jose watches her cut the third piece out of the corner of his eye. Then. Then the knife falls to the floor. What has frightened her? Why are her eyes so wide with fright? Jose hurries to the kitchen, his crooked body swinging on its cruel axis. He feels the strain of speed pulling at his spine.

"Ma'am. What is wrong?"

She is shaking her head. She is pale as a ghost. He would like to hug her then, tell her not to worry. He would like to take her by the hand to sit her in a chair in the living room.

"Ma'am," he says again, "what is wrong?"

She sees him finally. In a quiet voice she says, "We must take the early bus home."

Shori has his gun. What is there to be afraid of? Not that he cares what this child thinks. This American had better be where she says he is. It's one thing to send a man over, it's another to have to go on your own. The ridiculous thing is that none of his men were available to apprehend this American because they were all out searching for him. Some would find that funny. Shori doesn't. At one point this was probably a beautiful house. There are paintings of fruit and flowers in the corners of the ceiling, but the ceiling is rotting. Everything rots in this country. The furniture is heavy and ornately carved, much of it with the letter G—that much he can recognize. There is a layer of dust on everything, and the corners are blunted by thick deposits of cobwebs. He follows the twin pigtails and narrow shoulders. Where could she be leading him? They walk through the kitchen. The floorboards creak beneath his weight. The child raises her two dark, round eyes and meets his in a most impolite and disquieting fashion. Shori sniffs. He achieves the nonchalant look of the truly uncomfortable. The child swings open the door. A staircase swoops down into the darkness.

The child raises her arm. She holds Shori firmly in her gaze, then gestures him downward.

"Bring him here," says Shori. He's not sure if the child understands the Japanese. Shori gestures up and out of the basement. He holds his ground.

The child looks at him, wide-eyed, angry.

Shori peers into the basement. He can't see an American down there. In fact, the basement's so dark that he can't see anything in there at all.

He feels two small hands hard at the base of his back.

He is plunged into darkness and his ankle is sending him distressing waves of pain. He is sitting on a dirt floor. What happened? There is no reasoning in this hellish country. He hears the jangle of a key trying to find resistance in a lock. Shori finds his gun and he points it about him; he can only articulate his fear in Japanese.

"I have a gun. I have a gun," he says to his invisible menace, the harsh breathing. This darkness makes the sound of his own breathing too loud, too harsh.

Mrs. Garcia is sure she saw Auring standing in the kitchen. Auring, her old nanny, who has been dead for close to a month. She stood clear as day there in the kitchen. She was wearing a faded pink dress that Mrs. Garcia remembered her favoring around the turn of the century. She said, "Baby, go home."

Mrs. Garcia waves a fly from her nose. It settles on her hand. She waves it off again, this time more vigorously, and watches it spiral upward toward the ceiling of the bus.

"Jose, why aren't we moving?"

"The driver's putting water in the engine."

Mrs. Garcia feels fear in the bottom of her stomach. She closes her eyes and watches the slow pools of purple erupt in the blackness. She would like to sleep for a year. She is that tired.

Shori's eyes struggle to focus. His ankle feels icy. The blood is pulsing in his ears. He holds his breath and hears a movement on the floor. A rat, maybe. This terrible country is full of them. He widens his eyes and, slowly, nameless shapes begin to emerge from the dark backdrop. His nostrils are dilated, like a wild animal's. He could be dead any second now. He could be killed, his guts ripped neatly from his belly by an angry, skeletal American right here in the bowels of this evil house. Shori can make out a doorway about ten feet from where he sits. Brighter shadows outline the rectangle of the door. Shori has never thought of darkness possessing degrees. He watches the shape slowly change as the door swings open on singing hinges. A small chair leans on the wall by the door. Shori wonders if he should get the chair to use as some form of protection, to use as a barrier between him and the unknown. Suddenly, the chair moves and begins creeping along the wall. Shori has lost it in the darkness. He hears the soft, light breathing of the figure. He raises the gun in the direction of the sound. Then, without warning, the figure appears between him and the doorway—a moment of revelation. Shori hears a crisp popping sound. He's moving across the floor, scooting back, still sitting. He breathes heavily. His right arm swings in wide arcs. Then all is quiet. His left hand is closed in a painfully tight fist. His right hand is closed around the gun. How many times has he fired? He isn't sure.

This is just a bus moving along a road flanked by rice fields. This is just an old woman with her disabled houseboy. She has been visiting her cousin, and is now rushing home. She will find her granddaughter dead in her basement. Shot. Two bullets in her head. She will find four other bullets pressed into the walls and beams of the basement. There will be a knife on the floor.

People will speculate for years. The kalesa driver will never forget the look on the girl's face, such determination. The whole thing just doesn't make sense. Why would this little girl want to lure Shori to the basement? What did she hope to achieve? Of course, Shori denies being there at all. The woman will not insist. She will not want the memory of Shori in her basement. She will not need that particular someone who took the life from her little granddaughter. She has enough villains to stand up for all her pain.

The bus rounds a curve, passes farmers and water buffalo. The sun hangs unblinkered in the sky. The dust clings to everything. The woman holds her bag in her lap. She covers her mouth with the back of her hand and blinks. A cold trickle of perspiration drips down the back of her calf. There is grit on her tongue and dust filming her teeth. The bus hits a bump, awakening her servant. He looks around, self-consciously. He wipes the saliva off his chin. In response to this, a young woman tugs at her skirt, forcing it to cover her knees. This bus juggles the passengers over bumps, around ditches. The driver clears his throat and sends a bulb of spittle flying out the window. He checks his rearview mirror. The image presented is the clear curving road, blue sky, green fields. This could be peacetime.

This could be any bus en route to any provincial town.

Order of Precedence

In the waning months of 1944, Harry Gillen found himself in Singapore, a resident of the prison camp at Changi. The camp had a dusty assembly area, several low-ceilinged, rat-infested barracks, and an overflowing pit of a latrine, where the fly population nested and hatched, rising to meet each new visitor with a cacophonous buzzing that reminded Harry of a brass band. All this was contained within a perimeter of chain-link fence topped with a coil of barbed wire. The guardhouse was raised by the gate, barring exit, which in turn was facilitated — in one sense — by the hospital. A Japanese colonel named Takashi lived in a whitewashed wooden bungalow bitterly watching as the war dragged on and he lost opportunity after opportunity for distinction. It was rumored that Takashi spent his evenings drinking copious amounts of confiscated English gin, but rumors were all Harry had to go on.

After three years of imprisonment, Harry considered himself basically the same, although possessing an entirely new perspective. His abominable hunger made him think about his beloved horses only as the occasion for stew, and Harry, once a heavy smoker, had now learned to chew leaves with bovine complacency. In fact everything from the once familiar past had in some way been translated to his current (and only) pastime: struggling against his slow starvation. He'd watched all his muscle shrink to bone. His mind too was shrinking. He imagined that his brain was now the size of a salted prune. Sometimes he remembered what it felt like to dress in the morning, the feel of starched underclothes, the divide of a sharp pleat running the length of his leg. Or even the way he nudged the underbelly of a horse with his boot heel during a polo match, how he pulled his shoulders back to get the spine long and flexible so that when the ball came his way, he was in good shape to reach and send it spinning beneath the straining muscle of the horse's neck. Sometimes Harry could meditate on a downpour as it thundered across the roof; he could translate it into galloping hoofs across the cantonment polo turf. And in the early mornings, if he could focus out the groaning of the dying and smell of the dead, he remembered the anticipation and excitement that happened in the brief coolness before the day blossomed into searing heat.

Harry had never considered fighting alongside the Japanese. He was aware of Subhas Chandra Bose's movement and the Indian National Army. Bose had originally tried to recruit Germany to help him rid India of the British, but in 1940 Germany was occupied with the war in Europe. Bose had found the Japanese more helpful. Indian National Army officers had shown up at Changi, but had only managed to recruit five thousand of the forty thousand Indian troops captured on Malaya. These men were now fighting the British in Burma. Harry had not been approached to enlist. He decided the Indian National Army thought him too British. And he was. Muslims and Hindus were as bad if not worse to the Anglo-Indians as the English. He'd cast his lot with the Raj, which at least aimed to do everything in the name of civilization. This loyalty had landed him in Singapore.

· · ·

Harry pinpointed the beginning of his ill fortune to a polo match at the start of the cool season. The day began inauspiciously. Over runny eggs, steak, and toast, Harry read about the latest developments in Africa. Outside the mess, he'd run into Tunsdale, who was still drunk from the night before, and because of this, was still in good shape. There was some fuss among the servants about a rabid dog. While Harry was smoking a cigarette he heard a shot. A couple of minutes later he saw the sweeper, broom in hand, rushing from the direction of the shot to the kitchen. Harry had asked about the shot and the sweeper, with his head bobbing in excitement, told Harry that the rabid dog was dispatched, midleap, going for the rifleman's throat. As worthy a target as any young tiger.

"I hope you're not going for the cook," Harry had joked. The sweeper thought that was very funny.

Harry looked up at the sun. He had to get a move on.

"I'm playing today," he told the sweeper, who wished him luck. Harry headed for the stables.

It was the start of 1941. The camp where Harry was stationed was a mere thirty miles outside of Calcutta, but this proximity meant little since the cantonment was a world unto itself; the camp had its own club and social life, and was completely autonomous. Calcutta was for the British memsahibs to go dress shopping and for the British officers to hunt for wives. Harry's regiment, the 11th Indian, was mostly a combination of British and Anglo-Indian officers, and sowars and sepoys recruited from the martial classes, dominated by Sikhs. The officers were all educated (the British at Sandhurst in England and the others at the Indian Military Academy at Dehra Dun) and a few were gifted horsemen. Once a month they played polo. Harry rented his horse from the army, but some of the wealthier fellows had their own, and the two teams were rounded out with the police chief, a local magistrate (who kept a half-dozen ponies, but preferred pig sticking), and a few Indian Civil Service men, all impeccably dressed and hesitant to get muddied.

There was little to do but sport, and if you didn't count drink, nothing to do but sport. The army-sanctioned, disease-free brothels were off limits to the Indians stationed there, and although Harry passed for European some of the time, if his blackness was to be discovered he would rather the discoverers weren't the drunken, sex-starved soldiers who seemed to frequent the *lal* bazaar. Rumors were circulating that the Japanese were making real trouble in China and would bleed into Burma in no time at all, but the only person who seemed to take the threat seriously was Subhas Chandra Bose (who was eager to have the British quit India) and he embraced it. On a day like this, with nothing looming but a polo match and the heavy drinking sure to follow, war was far from Harry's mind.

Harry found his horse brushed and ready. He insisted on saddling her himself, despite the protesting groom, then walked her over to the polo field so as not to tire her out. Major Berystede arrived later with two horses, riding a third mount. Each of the horses had its own turbaned syce to minister to its needs. An attendant carrying mallets and a boot brush stood by, his expression impassive, his clothes immaculate. Couches lined the east perimeter of the field, on which an assortment of hatted, white-stockinged English ladies and their small children had arranged themselves. Waiters with silver trays propped gracefully on the left hand ministered lemonade with the right. A large tree on the west perimeter was quickly filling up with barefooted children.

On Harry's team were the pig-sticking magistrate, Captain McCaffrey, on a black Australian pony, and the local sanitation officer. On the opposing team were Major Berystede; a senior Indian Civil Service officer whom Harry recognized from the camp but didn't know; the venerable Colonel Corning; and Lieutenant Ruff, who was very young and very well connected. Harry was beyond doubt on the better team. Berystede, despite his enthusiasm and entourage, could seldom give his fellow players more than an outraged "Stop sticking your elbow into my ribs, you barbarian." His other team members were competent and that was all. In contrast, Captain McCaffrey was a ferocious player, drinker, and soldier. The magistrate was equally fierce. And the local sanitation officer had a chip on his shoulder owing to his nickname, "Toilet-wallah."

One short hour later, the match was over.

In the course of the match, Harry scored six of the eight points for the losing team. Apparently Berystede had complete disregard for right of way, but this was not of interest to the umpires. Neither was Berystede's menacing the magistrate's horse with his mallet, nor his galloping right at Harry, whooping like a crazy Afghan, which had unsettled Harry's horse. Twice the game had been stopped so that Ruff could retrieve his mallet from where he'd dropped it. This had occasioned McCaffrey to yell something that had the words "mother" and "tit" in the same sentence, and although the umpires never determined precisely what had been said to the young lieutenant, they'd awarded Ruff a penalty, which—miracle of miracles—had scored a goal.

Harry was angry with himself for even entertaining thoughts of victory. He smiled the stiff smile of a good sportsman. There was a smattering of applause as the men left the field, ladies winging their pale hands together, the clapping of the dead. Simultaneously, a gathering of crows clattered off the ground and settled into the tree where the children had been and now were not. The sun was larger in the sky, whiter than yellow, and Harry's shadow was pooled around the soles of his boots.

Harry's pony had an ugly cut on her right forefoot, but on closer inspection, the cut was bloody rather than deep. He was covered in dust and some muscle in his right hand was twitching painfully, a result of the grip on his mallet. He was ready for a drink.

"Lieutenant Gillen, do you want my syce to have a look at

that?" It was Major Berystede, who still looked remarkably clean.

"Sir?" said Harry.

"That cut. It might not look like much, but an open wound like that in this climate . . . You wouldn't want it to get infected."

"I'd appreciate that very much." Harry smiled and slapped the horse's shoulder.

"Where's your second horse?"

"Borrowed," said Harry, "from the magistrate."

"That's a fine mount, there."

"Not so fine, but she gets the job done, and for that she has my respect."

"Yes," said the major, "good is as good does. Performance is the key. I think, perhaps, we British put too much stock in breeding."

Harry controlled his smile. The major had just put his foot in his mouth. Harry ran his hand down the horse's leg and squeezed the fetlock, pretending to inspect the hoof.

"Breeding horses, that is. And horses are what we're talking about. Horses. Yes. And we breed dogs."

"Sir," said Harry, looking up. The major's face was a brilliant red. "I appreciate your offer. I feel I'm delaying you. I'd be delighted to continue the conversation at the mess after we've both had a chance to bathe."

"Absolutely. I'm buying the first round."

Harry had the first round in the shower. The water thundered over his head and that, accompanied by the slow, even burn of whisky down his throat, was hard to equal.

After his shower, Harry dressed quickly. Harry's grandfather had said that Harry could ride all the way to colonel on the back of a polo pony. Maybe he was right. Rather than entering the dining room through the long corridor, Harry slipped out the back, letting the screen close silently behind him. He needed a private smoke before he faced the major. He needed time to remember who he was in the army—Lieutenant Gillen, reserved,

elegant, somewhat mysterious as many Anglo-Indians were—
rather than the conflicted, cynical man that the last few months
of drinking and horse sport had created. Harry reminded himself that he was lucky to be in the army, better than the ICS with
its excruciating exam and cramped offices. What else would he
do other than soldier? India for Anglo-Indians was the ICS and
the army. Except for the Indian railways. And who wanted to
work on a train?

Harry tossed his cigarette to the ground. Behind the mess was
an impressive mango tree, whose branches stretched over the
whole compound. In the right season, the tree blushed red when
the green fruit ripened. Monkeys clattered through the branches,
waving their bony, lax fingers at each other in angry bargaining.
Birds sang in low, then shrill, keys and the leaves shivered with
life when a breeze crossed the cantonment.

A respectful distance from the mess back door, a boot-wallah
in his yellowed headcloth and coarse robe was abusing a boot to
a brilliant sheen with a camel-hair brush. A few bursts of conversation and an occasional gruff laugh came from the dining
room. Harry took out another cigarette. He was about to light it
when he caught the boot-wallah surreptitiously watching him.
He returned the cigarette to the case. Major Berystede was waiting for him and despite the beautiful stillness of the early afternoon, Harry had a duty to perform, even if it was in the form of a
few drinks and some idle conversation.

The major was a moderate drinker, which was a nuisance because Harry was not. He had to pace himself while watching the
slow erosion of Berystede's ice cubes, the sorry dilution of fine
whisky.

"You're a local boy, aren't you, Harry?"

"Not far from here. Serampore."

"It must be nice to be near home."

"I spent most of my childhood at boarding school. I know
more about Jubbulpore than about my home town."

"You went to Christ Church?"

"Yes, sir."

"None of that sir, sir in the mess, Harry. Call me Edgar."

"Edgar." Harry skidded his chair a few inches closer, not to be intimate, but to place himself directly under the electric fan, which was churning the smoky air with a desperate chug-chug. He glanced quickly at the bar, where Tunsdale waggled his eyebrows at him and raised a tumbler.

"And what business is your father in?"

Harry took out his cigarette case. "Unfortunately, my father is dead. But my grandfather is quite alive." He tapped a cigarette on the case. "We're in jute."

"Yes. Fine stuff, that."

"My grandfather says that he owes much to war and that having me in the military is somehow settling his debt."

"How's that?"

"Jute is fine stuff, true, but it became profitable during the Great War when it was needed to make sandbags."

Berystede responded with a gruff "Haw, haw."

At the bar, Tunsdale was balancing a cigarette on his forehead. No doubt, someone now owed him a drink. Harry looked back to the major. The major was studying Harry's face, the aquiline nose, the deepset hazel eyes, the anomalies that made Harry untouchable and handsome.

"Gillen . . . Is that Scottish?" asked Berystede.

"My grandfather is from Aberdeen."

"And your mother?"

"From Goa, a Christian. She met my father while vacationing in Simla."

"And I'm all English," said Berystede, leaning in. "Although I think there's a lot to be said for cross-breeding, hybrid vigor and the like." The major signaled a waiter for another round and Harry realized that the reason he drank so lightly was that liquor went straight to his head. "Take you, for example," he said. "The finest horseman in the area." Berystede leaned back into the cushion of his chair. His pale blue eyes narrowed. Harry knew the conversation had taken a direction. "Harry," said the major, "have you ever thought of joining the club?"

"The club?" Harry composed his features and his head moved to one side. "I can't say that I have."

"Well, why not?"

"With all due respect, although I am often termed a European I am undeniably Indian."

"The club takes Indians. We voted on it six months ago."

"I'm aware of that, sir. However, how many Indians are members?"

"You'd be the first one."

Harry rattled his ice cubes. "I am intrigued."

"You are polite. You're wondering why I'm so determined to make you a member."

"I'll ask you civilly," said Harry and smiled. "To what do I owe this honor?"

"Honestly? You owe this honor to polo. We lack the numbers and you're the best player at camp."

Harry nodded a couple of times. Berystede's earnest, vulnerable face was gratifying and for a moment Harry toyed with the idea of telling the major that he wasn't interested, not at all, in joining the estimable club.

Harry waited in line for water with an Australian named Smalls. Three years in Changi had transformed Smalls from an already wiry man into a knot of leather and bile. Smalls was Harry's closest friend. Harry found little to like about him, but Smalls took survival for granted, and in that he was singular. He also maintained a healthy anger and could find a responsible party for any indignity or pain, which made prison life seem less of a series of divine slights. For example, the tinea that had first ravaged Harry's feet, then buckled his nails until they dropped off. The fungus had lodged in his testicles where it burned and itched, making him sleep only in fits. There was fungus on his scalp and under the foreskin of his penis. The itch was so constant and uniform that Harry began to hear it buzzing in his ears. This buzzing itch had quickened his heartbeat and was unseating his brain.

"I've got the Changi balls too," said Smalls. "Fucking Poms."

"You blame the English for that?" asked Harry.

"And who do you blame? Who sent you here? Who gives a shit if there are Japs in Singapore?"

Harry nodded.

"There are Singapore slanty-eyes and Jap slanty-eyes. What's the bloody difference?"

"You're angry."

"I'm alive," Smalls said. He seemed to find the complacency of the dead offensive.

Four hours passed and Harry was still squatting in the sun.

The guard in charge of overseeing the distribution of water had disappeared without explanation. Now, all the prisoners in line were quiet and vigilant. Three men had already been carted off, dead or nearly dead. Harry's tongue was thick in his throat and he breathed with short breaths through his nose. His hands were folded over his head to shield him from the sun. He had meditated himself into a half-wakeful state in order to conserve energy and was rocking very slowly back and forth on his heels, which he thought helped his circulation. The man in front of him, whom he recognized but did not know, had blood dripping through his loincloth onto the baked dirt. Harry had closed his eyes because the redness of the man's blood made him dizzy. He wondered if the man contemplated his imminent death, whether he took it for granted.

The sound of a truck grinding up to the gate stirred Harry and he looked, squinting, over at the guards swinging the gate open. The sun was brilliant on the barbed wire, glittering in places like earthbound stars. No. The stars were in the space of air just before Harry's eyes. He would soon pass out and if he did that, he might not get water and there was a strong likelihood that this would be his last memory of life. The truck entered the compound. The engine was shut off and then the tailgate dropped with a screech and boom. Harry turned his head with effort. More prisoners. More men. He watched as they lowered themselves from the back of the truck, aware of their fragility yet poised and fluid, worried about attracting the attention of the guards. Harry hazarded a deep breath. The last of the men descended the truck, a small thin man in a loincloth with a fringe of gray hair, on his beaky nose a pair of wire glasses, and for one moment Harry thought he saw the radical Gandhi. He shut his eyes briefly. It was no hallucination. The man was still there, but it was not Gandhi. No. The man in the loincloth and glasses was Major Berystede.

"Move on, Harry," said Smalls, who was poised at his shoulder. "Move on." The guard had returned to the pump and slowly the coils of waiting men moved forward.

Harry knew there was no room for mistakes. He could not slip up. A careless word here or there would be failure. A dirty cuff or a missing stud and it was over. He would have to make it through dinner, drinks, and maybe a game of poker. He would be scrutinized the whole time. The members then voted by writing a ball beside their names—a white ball would mean acceptance, a black ball rejection. But how much could Harry care about all of this? He could see his face reflected in the toe of his shoe, which struck him as extravagant and ridiculous. He remembered how his grandfather had made him jog up and down the driveway in bare feet to toughen him up, to save him from his mother's "oily sweetness." But even his grandfather, opinionated and coarse, with curls of hair in his nostrils and ears, whose temper sent the servants scurrying and his wife into silent fury, even he would find Harry's membership impressive. A victory for Harry would be a victory for all Anglo-Indians. Despite the fact that Harry did not see himself as a victim, he had faithfully cataloged the many slights against him: playful references to his "touch of the tar," the awkward moments at the end of the evening when his British friends retired to the white-only brothel and he to his room, the English girl he had met while at Christ Church who had thought him fine to fool around with, but not to take home. Harry took a deep breath and went to the mirror to finish his hair.

The table had been set according to the Order of Precedence, which meant Harry was way down at the end, but thankfully close to Tunsdale, who was also a lieutenant. Someone's young nieces had shown up to tour India and were seated to Harry's left and across the table. The blond one seemed both exceedingly young and exceedingly stupid. She stared openly at Harry, as did her dark-haired sister, who was older and, although not much more than twenty, somehow past her prime.

"Harry's a great polo player," said Tunsdale. "He's also a lot of fun."

"What's that?" asked Major Berystede, who sat farther up, appropriately seated between the wife of a senior Indian Civil Service officer and an engineer.

"More polo," said Mrs. Berystede, who was seated across and two seats down from the major. "I prefer hunting."

"The major's wife is an excellent shot," said Tunsdale.

"And hunter," continued Mrs. Berystede. "In fact, I've been hunting in India for so long that I prefer jackal to fox. I think they run better."

This last statement was met with some approval.

"Is it true," said the blond-haired girl, addressing Harry, "that Indians keep harems?"

"Not a harem in the Arab sense of the word," Harry said, smiling in studied calm, "but often the women are kept out of sight and in the past more wife than one was permitted."

"Is it true," she continued, "that Indians burn young widows?"

"Oh shut up, please," said her sister. "I'm sorry. I apologize on her behalf."

"No, don't do that," said Harry. "I prefer when people say what they're thinking. How else can we understand each other?" The table had hushed silent to hear Harry's response. "The practice to which you refer is suttee, which is now illegal thanks to a law introduced by the British and quickly embraced by a majority of Indians." True or not, it was the appropriate thing to say. It occurred to Harry that this ignorant girl had been seated by him precisely for the members to gauge his performance under pressure. He waited for her to approach the topic of the Quit India movement, to ask him what he thought of England's shameless draining of India's resources, the mayhem that would follow their (hypothetical) withdrawal. But the girl, like the majority of people seated at the table, was blissfully unaware of the movement or didn't think it table-worthy conversation. Which was fine with Harry, because on this point, as with everything that made him choose between India and England, he was deeply conflicted.

After dinner, Harry thought that he had earned a cigarette on his own. There were people on the veranda and Tunsdale had only just left him to go to the bathroom, so Harry did not feel the need to engage in another conversation just yet. But he was not so lucky. Berystede's jackal-slaying wife was quickly shortening the distance between them, glass raised, and in Harry's judgment, a little unsteady on her feet.

"Harry," she said, "may I call you Harry?"

"Of course," said Harry.

"And I'm Christina and you may call me Mrs. Berystede or Major Berystede's wife." She laughed. "I'm so sorry that we are so horribly boring and pretentious."

Harry smiled nervously. "I haven't judged you so harshly."

"You'd think we could do better in this club," she said.

"Better?"

"I mean, you're the first Indian we've even considered, and you're the whitest Indian I've ever seen." Mrs. Berystede flagged the waiter, who pretended not to see her and continued to another group. "Damn," she said, "let's go inside and get a drink."

"I'll follow you as soon as I finish this," said Harry, raising his cigarette, "in the moonlight."

Mrs. Berystede nodded pleasantly, then plowed inside, passing Tunsdale in the doorway.

"Well, she's got good strong legs, a full set of big, white teeth, and a nicely shaped head," said Tunsdale under his breath. "She'd make a fine horse."

Harry closed his eyes. "They're not going to make me a member."

"If they do, wonderful. If they don't, to be honest, in your position I'd have more fun bicycling through a minefield."

Harry smiled. Tunsdale was right. Not only did Harry not belong in the club, but he also felt no sadness at being the outsider. He tossed his cigarette off the veranda and watched it burn briefly before it was extinguished. One day this club would be nothing but a queer memory. Now it was no more than a laughable reality.

Harry went inside to find the major and indulge in some safe horse talk. The members were gathered in clusters, rattling ice, sweeping smoke in exaggerated gestures as if involved in an elaborate ritual to ward off the passage of time. The major was nowhere to be seen and Harry accidentally made eye contact with the dark-haired, chain-smoking niece. Harry suspected she'd been sent to India as a last-ditch effort to get her married.

"Lieutenant Gillen," she said, "I'd love to hear about the real India."

Harry steeled himself for a discussion of elephants. He sat down on a two-seater couch a comfortable distance from the girl's chair. She put the cigarette between her thin lips and exhaled in angry, staccato puffs.

"I was on a hunt last week and fell into a creek. Can you imagine?" She seemed disgusted by this, but somehow expected Harry to be charmed. "My whole right side is sore and I've got a terrible gash on my shin."

Harry was trying to decide whether it was courteous or indecent to look at the girl's shin, when Mrs. Berystede showed up unexpectedly and sank down onto the couch next to him. Her knee bumped his and her drink spilled in a dark purple patch on the front of her lavender dress.

"My fault," said Harry quickly. He pulled out his handkerchief and handed it to her.

"Thank you," she said. She dabbed at herself in a casual way and her body relaxed against Harry's. Harry edged himself onto the perimeter of the couch so that the majority of his weight was balanced on the balls of his feet. He had to turn to look at her at a pivot, over his shoulder. She looked in her glass and rattled the ice. "This evening has the smell of death," she said, "or maybe I'm just mortally bored."

Harry laughed and allowed himself to look at her. Mrs. Berystede was not pretty, not even handsome. Her nose was too big and her chin just a dimple in her jaw on the way to her neck, but she had lovely eyes, large and expressive and somehow, despite her wit, sad.

"Do you have a family, Harry?" she asked.

"Not of my own. I have two brothers and one sister."

"What do they do?"

"My older brother is in the railways. My younger brother is in training for the Civil Service. And my sister is mad about archery and jazz. She does the books for the family business."

"Oh, that's wonderful." Mrs. Berystede's hand went to Harry's shoulder. "I want a family," she said. "Edgar tells me that I am mother to all of India. Why do I need a baby when I am mother to six hundred million people?" Mrs. Berystede began to tear up and the handkerchief strayed to her eyes. Her voice dropped to a whisper. "Of course Edgar tells everyone that it's me, but I've been to the doctor. I just get so angry." The tears began to spill, but she managed a smile. "I want to shoot everything in sight."

Harry nodded, then raised his glass to Mrs. Berystede and drained it. He wished he could put his arm around her. "I can tell you are a good woman," he said, "and I'm sure that you would be a wonderful mother. I am sorry."

"Oh," said Mrs. Berystede, sitting suddenly straight, "you are so kind."

There was a silence in the room. Harry looked up and an informal assembly was watching him. He was not surprised. In the front row was a shocked Major Berystede. Behind him and to the left was Tunsdale, who was smiling with support and sympathy. Harry knew he had just been unanimously blackballed.

Tunsdale and Harry rode back to the cantonment together. "What an outright disaster," said Tunsdale. "I haven't had that much fun at the club since I joined. What was the old bag telling you, anyway?"

"Nothing of interest," said Harry. "She was just a bit lonely."

"And wanted the company of the handsome, swarthy lieutenant."

"She's right to be crazy here," said Harry. "It shows the presence of—"

"Of what?"

"Of a soul," said Harry and they laughed.

The next morning Harry awoke to both the sting and blur of a headache. The walls were spinning around the room and his attendant, although studiously solemn, had a merry twinkle in his eyes.

"I feel terrible," Harry confided. "Give me some water." Harry sipped cautiously from the edge of his glass. His stomach was very delicate.

"Sir," said his servant. He gestured around the bridge of his nose and Harry hazarded to touch the cheekbone beneath his left eye, which was throbbing. The flesh around his eye was swollen and tender.

"Is it bruised?" asked Harry.

"Quite black," said his servant. "It looks very painful."

"Wonderful," said Harry.

With some effort and a good deal of help from his servant, Harry managed to get dressed and shaved. His mind kept flashing images at him — Tunsdale handing him his flask, the ensuing argument, Tunsdale and Harry at the army brothel (Harry fortified into feeling one hundred percent European), and the one knuckle-up punch from the unidentified fist, which had sent him flying right back into the arms of Mother India. Tunsdale had tried to pass Harry off as Welsh, despite the fact that all the men frequenting "the rag" knew him. In fact, Harry had been laughing when the punch hit him and even though his head was reeling and he had more pains than one, he chuckled to himself as he crossed the swept dirt of the garden and made the steps of the mess.

He didn't even notice Berystede smoking on the veranda.

"Lieutenant," said the major.

"Sir," said Harry.

"What on earth happened to your eye?"

"This, sir?" Harry shook his head. "The lesser part of honor." Which was indiscretion.

Berystede stiffened. "You should put some ice on it," he said.

Harry nodded and continued inside.

How was Harry to know that at the same time Tunsdale was insisting that he was Welsh, Berystede and his wife had finished off a monumental, tight-lipped row. When Harry was struggling back onto his horse, Mrs. Berystede too was mounting hers, taking off for an angry moonlight ride across the fields. While Harry was passed out in bed with his servant easing off his boots,

Mrs. Berystede had just pitched off her horse while flying over a ditch. When she finally returned home she was cut, muddied, and humiliated. She refused to offer an explanation. Berystede had not slept that night and the sight of Harry, smelling distilled, handsome despite his obvious lack of sleep, strong, young, and vital, had stirred his deepest insecurities.

And Harry's explanation for the state of his eye had planted the seeds of suspicion.

Tenko, Japanese reveille, came at the end of the night. Changi was run on Japanese time, even though Singapore was an hour and a half behind. Harry was dreaming of some mountain-edge horse game where the players leaped one after another, gleefully, spiraling downward and never hitting bottom. He rolled to his feet out the side of the cot as Sergeant Itsumi plowed down the row of the sleeping men, pounding their shins with his flashlight. Today was a lucky day because all the men managed to get to their feet. All had survived the night. Outside, the sky was just starting to glow with the coolest, most distant light. *Bango* started and the men counted off dutifully in Japanese: *ichi, ni, san, shi, go . . .*

"*Roku!*"

. . . shichi, hachi, ku, ju . . .

Berystede was not a dream. Harry had seen him, recognized him, despite three years' wear and alteration. Probably Berystede was in the hospital. Harry had watched him walk from the truck toward the assembly area until he disappeared behind the edge of the barracks. He had watched the determined limp, the pained grimace, and felt sad to see him so low. Only the major's supposed death had made Harry reconsider his contempt, but now . . . Berystede was old and weak, neither dead nor alive, and Harry was unable to articulate his emotion.

After breakfast, Harry went to the hospital to have the doctor dust his genitals with sulfur. The hospital was a long hut with a few low cots and a number of mats laid edge to edge. Harry paused outside the door, arrested by the metallic stench of warm blood. At the screen, two dozen flies buzzed angrily to get in, while just inside the same number were trying to escape. The major was indeed there, lying on a mat, one arm thrown out onto the floor, the fingers curled in a loose fist. Harry watched the major sleep as he endured the stinging shock of the sulfur and the doctor's sympathetic fanning, which the doctor performed with his broad-brimmed hat.

"Open your mouth for me," said the doctor.

Harry obliged.

"Jesus Christ. You've still got all your teeth. Have you been eating insects?"

"Yes, sir, per your recommendation." Harry leaned in and whispered, "The major, is he all right?"

"I'm afraid not. It's a miracle he made it here."

"Can I talk to him?"

"Do you know him?"

"Yes."

Harry went to squat beside the major's mat. The flesh on Berystede's face had been eaten away and his lips were dry, pulling up on his teeth so that his gums were exposed. When the major breathed, a shallow, rasping sound escaped his mouth, the same sound a shell made when you put it to your ear. Clearly, Berystede was sleeping, but his eyes were open a crack and the whites showed, although the irises quivered into view.

"Major Berystede," whispered Harry, "it's Lieutenant Gillen, sir."

The eyes shuddered open.

"Lieutenant Gillen," he repeated.

Berystede took a deep breath, "Harry. You look well."

Harry nodded.

"So," the major's face relaxed, "I finally found a club that would take us both."

· · ·

Malaya had been an unqualified disaster.

The 11th Indian were garrisoned at Sitra on the west coast of Malaya, after pulling back from the Siamese border. They were to hold the Japanese here, where there was a road heading south. The Japanese force was inferior in numbers and, Harry had been told, in strength. The Japanese were all nearsighted. They couldn't aim a rifle. Their legs were bowed so that they scampered when upright in a half-evolved netherworld between ape and man. At their tallest, the Japs hit four feet. They had bucked, protruding teeth. They spat when they talked. Fighting them was presented as an indignity to be suffered. Harry wondered that they hadn't left for Malaya armed with a sack of rat poison. The first night, when they were still organized with the men sleeping in their regimental rows and a separate officers' latrine, Harry had been unable to sleep. The English were wrong about the Japs. They were as formidable as any Germans, Boers, or Afghans. Harry knew this, just as he knew that the Indian part of his blood boiled equally with the British.

On December 12, 1941, the soldiers of the 11th Indian, after suffering major losses, began their retreat from Sitra. Three days later, the 11th Indian had been pushed south forty kilometers to the village of Gurun. The supposedly pro-British villagers had refused them food and while Major Berystede made a ridiculous speech about crown and colony, Harry, Tunsdale, and the others "confiscated" as much food as they could. Harry no longer knew whom he was protecting or even why he was fighting, aside from some abstract sense of right and wrong, British perfection and Japanese barbarism.

Two days later, a flanking move by Japanese ground forces had split the British and Commonwealth troops up the middle. Japanese air strikes had forced Harry and the others into the jungle. The 11th Indian was lost. Harry was one of a band of forty men—separated and hungry—trying to navigate back to the coast. For four days they retreated through solid, snake-infested jungle. While they were wading through a waist-deep creek, sunk to the knees in mud, a steady rain of bullets began to fall and Harry had watched more than twenty men die right there. He'd watched their bodies sinking slowly. The Japanese were silent, efficient, and invisible, nothing more than a singing bullet and rustle of jungle greenery.

None of the 11th Indian were trained in jungle warfare. Some of the older men had been in Shanghai, but their withdrawal from the "Paris of the East" in 1937 had not prepared them for this. Harry had thought through the surrender of Shanghai. If the Japanese were so insignificant, then why had the British surrendered? He had heard other officers explaining this embarrassment away, saying that Hong Kong was more valuable, that the British did not want to provoke the Japanese when the naval base at Singapore, Changi, was still in the process of construction. But the truth of the matter was that the British had no more right to be in Shanghai than the Japanese and with Chiang Kai-shek agitating against imperial forces — Japanese and British — withdrawal was the only sensible move. At least an organized, urban withdrawal was something that the Indian army was well equipped to execute.

The Australian troops, also there at the request of Mother England, had outright laughed at Harry and his men, their kits, their swords, the ceremonial panache with which they approached soldiering. The Indian army was trained to give and take orders, but in the jungle you could not see or hear the commanding officer and the situation changed so rapidly that one needed initiative and confidence to act independently, two traits that had been systematically drilled out of the soldiers' mindset. The jungle made the men crazy. The sky only revealed itself in slivers, the invisible sun only served to raise steam into the air. Harry's proud sepoys, mostly from the plains of the Punjab, were reduced to struggling on all fours.

Major Berystede led what was left, maybe twenty men, up a

rocky creekbed. Progress was slow because of the injured, and Harry was relieved when after four hours' march, the ground began to level out. Through the dense greenery ahead, Harry could see bright light, which threw all the great leaves and sinewy vines into relief. They were at the edge of the jungle. When Harry's platoon burst through the last of the tropical growth, they found themselves at the perimeter of a clay tennis court. It was as surprising as Alice's tumble into Wonderland. Suddenly the sun shone in an acceptable, general way. Birdsong was loud and lovely, without the crash and startle of branches breaking overhead. Beyond the tennis court was a handsome house with a wide veranda and classic columns. Papaya and banana trees grew in attractive clusters bordered with whitewashed rocks and there was a faint smell of blossoms. The lawn, until very recently, had been meticulously maintained.

Harry stepped onto the court. He listened. The place was completely silent, something that made him uneasy. Major Berystede cautiously peered around. He sheltered his eyes with his hand and squinted up at the house. He seemed lost and Harry knew what was running through his head: he couldn't even keep track of men he'd lost and didn't want to make any more decisions that would result in more death.

"I'll go on ahead," said Harry.

Harry's heels sounded lightly on the clay court. Only recently, someone had swept it smooth, because the clay was even except for one disturbed path up through the center. Harry squatted down to look at the tracks—small men's feet and, if he wasn't mistaken, cloven, the toes separated, the prints wide.

"Lieutenant Gillen!"

Harry turned.

It was Sergeant Singh, standing not quite at attention, but not quite at ease.

"Come on then," said Harry, "let's go find this devil." Harry got up and they approached the house together, walking in clear sight of whatever had silenced it. The sound of the major's voice drifted across the court and lawn—soothing and low—as he organized search parties to the right and to the left of the garden. The heat was only just starting and Harry's mind wandered from thoughts of battle and blood.

"I find it very strange," said Sergeant Singh, "a lovely house like this in the middle of the infernal jungle."

Harry nodded, then raised a hand to quiet him. Together, carefully, they mounted the steps. The door hung open on its hinges and when pushed, swung noiselessly inward. Harry followed the arc of it and found himself in a foyer with a parquet floor and a cathedral ceiling. At the top of the curving stairs was a rose window. A small brown sparrow was trapped there and beat itself against the brilliant panes. Beams of light splintered through the glass onto the landing in an exact rose pattern, disturbed only by the bird, whose desperate shadow marred the perfect symmetry. Harry continued to his right, where the sound of an electric fan and some rustling papers asserted itself against the quiet. Together, Harry and Sergeant Singh walked across the waxed floors and through the arch that marked off a library—a white-walled room with a large bay window fitted with velvet bench seats, floor to ceiling shelves with books bound in red leather and blue cloth, an old pukka once used to move air still on the ceiling, and a broad blackwood desk with the electric fan blowing the papers of a ledger to a desperate flutter. And at the desk, wearing the pocket jacket favored in Malaya, his pale hands still resting on the table, was the presumed owner of the house. Harry was surprisingly unmoved. The man was dead, clearly, because the neck terminated in a clean, fresh wound. The man's head was nowhere in sight.

"I have heard of this," said Sergeant Singh.

"Yes," said Harry.

Then the spattering noise of gunfire reached them across the yard, the hearty shouts of men (like a football game), and the screech of a bird.

"Why weren't you and the major captured together?" Smalls asked. He and Harry were again in line, this time for food. Harry had an old sardine can for a bowl, a spoon cut from beaten tin. The sun was still hot and high. Past the fence, the column of bearers carried out the daily dead, slung between them in sheets. Harry breathed deeply and raised a hand to his forehead.

"Well," said Harry, "Sergeant Singh and I heard the shots. The Japanese didn't know we were there. Sergeant Singh and I went out the back door." Harry remembered the open pit by the clothesline, the little boy flung face up, his mother's shoeless but stockinged foot. "We were outnumbered. I had an idea that later, when it was dark, the sergeant and I would free some men, create a disturbance." There was Tunsdale again with his hands tied, towering over his Japanese captor. And there was Tunsdale crumpling, his intestines unraveling onto the wet earth, the bayonet greased with his blood. "We had no opportunity. I thought if we could find more men . . ."

"Well," said Smalls, "did you?"

"Yes," said Harry. "And here we all are."

Harry did not know what had compelled him to visit Major Berystede the last two days. He did not know what comforted him in their uneasy truce.

With the remnants of the 11th Indian struggling on the Malay Peninsula, the major had seen endless opportunities to rid himself of the embarrassment of Lieutenant Gillen and he had taken all of them. More than once Harry had caught the major eyeing him with a look somewhere between fear and guilt. Harry dryly noted that he was being singled out either for heroism or death. Only the hand of fate would make it clear which of these it was to be, so Harry was first at the mercy of a capricious man and, after that, an even more capricious God.

Harry had been ordered to lead a group of men up a slope to a makeshift bunker the Japanese had set into a hillside. The line of greenery broke abruptly to a smooth ascent. There wasn't much on this side of the hill, but scouts had come back with descriptions of a series of fields on the other side, already strewn with their dead. The major had decided to take the bunker and he had decided that Harry would do it, just as yesterday he had decided that Harry was the best man to run a message to Lieutenant Colonel Lifkin, which involved a good two-hundred-meter sprint through a papaya grove, whose slim trunks and umbrella foliage offered little protection from snipers. Harry tried to control himself, but he hadn't slept in days and had never been much good at anything but feigned deference. The men were checking their rifles, whispering requests to their respective deities. Harry approached Major Berystede and asked in a low voice, "Excuse me, sir, but I must ask you, are you trying to kill me?"

"Lieutenant Gillen . . ."

"I apologize. A voice inside keeps telling me this is none of my business. But surely it is."

Berystede was taken aback. "What kind of insubordination is this?"

"Some variety, but at this rate I'll be dead by sundown, so the chances of my being court-martialed are very slim."

The major was rattled. He inhaled deeply. "Are you refusing to execute the order?"

Harry thought about it for a minute. "No, sir."

But despite the major's best efforts, it hadn't been Harry's time. The bunker was empty, the battle already won by the Japanese, the field deserted.

• • •

From the look on the doctor's face, Harry knew the major was close to death. Berystede's eyes brightened when he saw Harry, as if all the troubles of the past were gone and Harry was still the handsome horseman, the major his eager patron, and the rumble of war an ugly rumor. Harry squatted by the cot and helped the major drink a little water, which was set on the crate along with the major's belongings—a worn photo of Mrs. Berystede on a horse, carrying a rifle, and a set of keys, one of which unlocked the liquor cabinet back in the mess hall at camp.

"Harry," said the major, "what are you going to do when you get home?"

"I don't know," Harry said.

"The English will all be gone."

"I find that hard to believe, sir."

"Please, call me Edgar."

"Edgar," Harry said, "you should probably sleep."

"I will sleep and sleep and sleep." The major smiled. His eyes were watering. Harry breathed deeply and took the major's hand. He'd done this on impulse and once he was holding it, didn't know how to put it down. The major's hand was cool, despite the thick heat. The bones were thin and fragile, like the skeleton of a bird. His skin already had the look of death. When the major finally drifted off, Harry set the hand down on the cot. Mrs. Berystede stared bravely out of the photograph from atop her horse, in approval of Harry's loyalty, or maybe deep disapproval of her husband's succumbing to his limitations. Harry would survive. He had no doubt about that. He would return to see how India had been altered by the war, as he too had been altered.

Outside, the sun slid down the sky, slipping through a cloud, touching the barbed wire. Harry hadn't told the doctor that the major was dead. Colonel Takashi was watching the sky. Harry thought he detected, in his posture, in the way his hand rested on the hilt of his sword, a nervousness. He realized then that the

Japanese were losing. He wondered if Smalls was still on work detail, if he'd made it back to the camp in one piece. Harry watched the dirt road, glowing in the final moments of the day, shining bright like the surface of a river.

There was a precise moment when Harry realized that he'd misjudged his battle. He had wrongly attributed the stakes. After Harry and Sergeant Singh had left the house, they pushed through the jungle for about four hours before hitting a dirt road. They rested there, unsure if they should risk the easy path, or if they should try their odds at surviving in the jungle. Maybe they could tough it out for a couple of weeks until Singapore was secure and the reinforcements arrived. Harry had been standing on the bank of civilization — the road, which gave no hint of its origin or terminus — when he heard a rattling, banging sound coming down the road. There was no rumble of engines, nor the sound of marching infantry, and the very strangeness of the noise froze him in place, until Sergeant Singh dragged him down. At the side of the road with his eyes level to its surface, Harry waited. A half minute later in a whir of pedals and wheels Harry saw a hundred Japanese flying down the road, a tight pack, all heavily armed and fortified. They were conquering the peninsula on bicycles.

"If we had our horses . . ." said Sergeant Singh.

But Harry heard no more. This was no place for horses, or English, or Indians. This was no place, only a dirt road that wound on and on, sinking heavily into its coils, crushing all in its path. This was a road with no origin or destination, just a brief breathing space in the heart of the jungle, a halting, a nothingness, that offered a limited view and a few hundred miles of packed dirt, meter upon meter, extending endlessly north and south without ever reaching home.

Guinea

MIDWAY THROUGH HIS TIME as a soldier, Francino found himself lost in the heart of the jungle. His companion was an Irishman from Boston named Burns and in their protection was a Japanese prisoner, starved beyond hope, who would most likely not survive the next two days. They wandered without the warmth of natural sun. The large leaves and woven canopy of the jungle ceiling filtered the light into a thousand gradations of shade. In this strange place, nothing was inanimate. Even the trees and rocks appeared to breathe.

The three men marched, not talking. The prisoner stumbled onward, scared and without will. Francino had let Burns decide to let the prisoner live. Francino did not like deciding the fate of other men any more than he liked contending with his own survival; his concerns were with the afterlife and how he was going to reconcile his current rifle-wielding life with God.

Maybe he had not suffered long enough, not like Burns who had been battling it out on active duty for eighteen months. This was the first Jap that Francino had seen close up—an emaciated soldier with his clothes rotted and a white loincloth visible through the seat of his shorts.

"If you'd seen more, you'd be dead by now," Burns told him. "In Guinea, a Jap close up is the last thing a man sees." Which made Burns sound wise, when he wasn't. Burns talked like the majority of the people Francino knew. He had a loud voice and an admirable sense of purpose, which was one of the perks war had for the unsophisticated. Francino listened for the thrum of engines in the sky, the powerful cough of machinery to cut through the billion singing insects. But there was no sound not intended by nature. Here, it was the Garden of Eden—primordial, pristine, unforgiving. Here, there was nothing to eat and Francino amused himself with the thought that if anyone offered food, even a snake holding an apple, he would take it and eat it—no questions asked.

But suffering was fine. He would be happy to get home in one piece.

On a plane trip to Sydney, Francino had found himself dozing off on his pack. An Australian soldier lay just beyond his head, on a stretcher. The Aussie was talking to someone farther off, whose voice Francino couldn't hear at all because the engine was too loud. Francino's eyelids were droopy with booze and fatigue, but the nasal voice of the Aussie on the stretcher kept him half awake.

"Yeah," the Aussie said, "the war's been a bit of disaster for me, you know?"

His companion must have said something.

"Yeah," said the Aussie, "me Mum's not gonna be too happy. I'm the only one left and riding a horse is gonna be a bit of a problem on account of me legs."

"Yeah," said the Aussie, "both of them. I wasn't too pleased about that."

"Yeah," said the Aussie, "Dad's not too fond of the Japs, and neither am I."

Francino fell asleep, with the Aussie's voice and his brilliant gift for understatement ringing in his ears, above the deafening drone of the airplane.

"Let's take a rest," said Francino. He nodded over at the prisoner, whose head was lolling onto his chest even though he was still walking. "I think we should untie his hands."

Burns held the rope which ran from the prisoner's wrists. "This is the only thing that's holding him up."

Francino sat with his back against the trunk of a tree. Burns was restless, looking back and forth. The Japanese soldier had passed out cross-legged, leaned against a rock. He looked like pictures Francino had seen of Peruvian mummies, who spent eternity sitting wrapped in blankets on a wind-swept desert plateau. Funny, he thought, how the dead who looked alive and the living who looked dead were similar in appearance.

"How long do you think we've gone today?" asked Francino.

"I'd guess around five miles."

Francino nodded to himself. What difference did it make if it was five miles in no particular direction? They had been wandering in the jungle for four days.

Francino and the entire 163rd Infantry had been in New Guinea since January. It was 1942. He'd witnessed Horri's startling advance across the Owen Stanley Mountains. He'd been a part of the effort that halted the Japanese in mid-September, and now he was pushing them back over the steep, punishing ridge. New Guinea was a great, sleeping alligator and the Owen Stanleys ran the length of her back. Sometimes, if you had a chance to be still and concentrate, you could feel the great beast heave beneath you in sweet, dreamless sleep.

The patrol had gone out on a Monday, at dawn. Mist was heavy in the air and the calls of birds sounded mere inches away, when they were really coming from the jungle ceiling. There were seven men, which was a lucky number, although Francino's lucky number was four. There were seven days in the week, seven seas. And seven deadly sins. Avarice. Lust. Gluttony. Sloth. Envy. Pride. And what else? A mosquito buzzed in his ear. Francino shook it off, rattling his gear. Burns, who was walking ahead of him, swung around. The end of Burns's rifle was in Francino's face.

Francino smiled. "Anger."

"What?"

"Anger. It's the seventh deadly sin."

Burns spat in response. Burns must have always been tightly wound and the war had rewarded this; Burns's superiors liked him, on the ready, alert. He was courting a mental breakdown. New Guinea was the perfect place for him. Burns was one of those men who would be made by war, whose last vestiges of childhood would be burned out of him bullet by bullet. People like Burns were grateful for such abundant, sanctioned violence. A month earlier, Francino might have felt sorry for him.

It was late October—fall—but in New Guinea things were green. It was as if that first startling instant of spring—when the trees started popping out little-fisted leaves and the ground was spongy with thaw—had been stalled and then expanded; the brief spring second here was repeated over and over, multiplied within itself and then replicated in a riot of leaves, steam, and fungus. The trees stretched against the very dome of sky. The air was compressed until it dripped down your face. Francino pushed his glasses back up his nose and the column drew to a halt. Sergeant Cole was nervous. He drank some water and squinted around at the men, even though the sunlight wasn't strong.

"I need a couple of scouts," he said.

Burns had volunteered and somehow it had been decided that Francino would join him. Francino couldn't figure out if Burns didn't like his hesitant manner or the fact that he was Italian or both. Burns wasn't too bright. At first Francino ignored him, but week after week in close quarters had worn down Francino's indifference. Their animosity had become undeniable.

Francino and Burns pushed through the undergrowth and circled around some kind of knoll. Francino looked to the edge of the trees. He and Burns had trampled a wide path. If there were Japanese hiding in the dense vines at the edge of the trees, Burns and he would see them, or evidence of them, from where they stood.

"What do you think?" asked Francino.

Burns cocked his head and looked off to the right. "I got a feeling."

Francino crouched deeper.

"But I can't hear nothing."

"Still . . ." Francino looked down to where the trees rimmed the vines. Cole had the other men moving carefully into the open. Francino could feel their unease. Cole, Frankel, Smith, Lescault, and Dove. The sun was beginning to burn through the mist.

Frankel was the first to fall. At first Francino thought Frankel must have hit some wire from the way his head jerked back and his stomach swung out. Francino was still trying to figure out what had happened when he felt Burns's hand hard on his arm pulling him down. Only then did Francino realize that he had stood up and was standing in clear view of whoever had felled Frankel. Then he was lying on his stomach. His rifle was ready although he wasn't. Burns was shooting at something saying, "Jesus, Jesus, Jesus." The target seemed to be moving. Francino tried to clear his mind.

A flying insect brushed his ear with her wings and Francino thought of the Angel of Death.

A purple, fist-shaped cloud hovered above him.

"Where are they?" yelled Burns.

Where were who?

There was sputtering fire below them. Someone (Lescault?) was screaming; he was hurt. But Burns and Francino were climbing. They were moving fast, like animals, on all fours. Burns moved ahead. Neither man spoke but Francino could hear each pull of Burns's breath, although his ears were filled with silence. They moved through the vines. The brush clattered and snapped. Small animals took to the trees, rattling branches high above them. Birds screamed in alarm. Francino scrambled under the trunk of a tree. The soles of Burns's boots were more worn on the inner edges and Francino tried to think if Burns was knock-kneed, but he could not remember. They moved upward still.

Burns, sweat pouring off his forehead, turned to Francino and said, "They let us go. They let us go because they knew we were scouts and that the rest of the squad would be moving behind us."

Francino's and Burns's safe passage had lured the other men into the open. Francino had never considered that, despite his confusion, he had been part of a plan. He was still dazed, under the impression that the two men had encountered a pocket of chaos, all of it accidental and beyond reason.

"We'll wait here," said Burns.

"Before we circle back and join the others?"

"The others? They're all dead."

Francino pondered this. "Then what will we wait for?"

Burns thought they should pick a direction and start walking, which was logical and dangerous for the same reason. The area had no clean battle lines; you could be at an Aussie checkpoint, continue on and find yourself face to face with the Japanese, only to fight your way through to the Dutch. They were on a checkerboard and at this point in the game, Burns wasn't sure whose square they were sitting on. Since their platoon had just been decimated, the area appeared to be under Japanese control. It was probably a good idea to move on and to move on soon.

"That's not a plan and I'm not a gambling man," Francino said to Burns.

"Then what are you? You're not much of a soldier."

Francino had responded with silence.

"I saved your life back there." Burns lifted his shoulders. "If it weren't for me, you'd be on your way back from New Guinea to Little Guinea."

Francino laughed. "I think I owe my life to the Japanese."

"To the Japs?"

"Yes," said Francino. "For missing."

Burns shouldered his rifle and spat. He nodded to Francino and Francino obliged. He walked over to their prisoner and shook him. The man woke up and struggled to his feet.

"We're moving," Francino said, then smiled to himself. He could have sworn that there was a flicker of recognition in the Jap's eyes, a resentment that betrayed an ego, someone not beaten down by fear. The man scuttled to his feet. Francino cut the rope on his wrists.

"He does anything, I'm holding you personally responsible," said Burns.

Francino looked at their prisoner. His eyes were watery, rimmed with yellow crust. "He's almost dead," said Francino.

Francino tried to stay alert, but his mind wandered and sometimes the sound of snapping twigs seemed too normal to pull out the usual register of noises. Maybe Burns was right. Maybe he was a bad soldier. Maybe he was too aware of what he was risking to be a good soldier. He kept thinking of Corporal Shedelsky after the bullet got him right above his left ear. Shedelsky had survived, but Francino found him late one afternoon wandering around in nothing but a pair of socks. Shedelsky had an umbrella, borrowed from a startled native who was watching with a nervous smile. Francino pictured himself dancing off a ship in his socks, his umbrella dangling, his sister and mother waiting open-mouthed. Head injuries scared Francino almost more than dying.

They'd taken the prisoner the day before. Francino's rifle had been propped against a tree and Burns was off attending to his fourth bodily function of the last hour. Despite his iron side, Burns lacked Francino's iron stomach. Francino was watching the progression of a column of ants along the jungle floor. He found himself naming them, starting with Cole and then Lescault. The ants were unaware of Francino. He gently placed a rock in the middle of their path, and they quickly circumvented it, with no thought to the cause of their detour. Francino leaned back from his squat into a sitting position. His socks were damp and he thought he should take them off and let his feet breathe for a while. He began to untangle his laces and had one of his boots half off when he heard Burns's low, frightened voice.

"Jesus," Burns said.

Francino looked up quickly. A Japanese soldier was standing no more than six feet from where he sat. His rifle was closer to the Japanese soldier than it was to him. Burns raised his rifle to the man's head.

"What are you doing?" said Francino.

Burns ignored him.

"What are you doing?" Francino repeated.

"Francino, I came here to kill some Japs."

"He's not armed."

The soldier slowly turned around. He looked to Burns, raising his hands in surrender.

"He's surrendering," said Francino.

"No, the Japs don't surrender. He's rigged."

"Rigged?"

"He's got a grenade or something. He's gonna blow himself up and us too."

Francino had managed to take his boot off at this point, and was now standing. He took a good look at the soldier, who was very thin and looked to be in his early twenties. His clothing was torn in patches and his eyes were milky, clouded.

"I think he's sick," said Francino.

"So what?"

"Save your bullet. If we can get him back to camp, he might be useful. He must have come from somewhere."

"And?"

"He's got to have some information."

Burns laughed. "You want to take him prisoner?"

"Yeah," Francino looked at the Jap. "Prisoner. Prisoner," he said. He clasped his wrists a few times mimicking handcuffs.

"Might make more sense if you did what the Japs do, just slice his head off. He'd understand that."

"I'm just following regulations. Either he's surrendering, or he's friendly. I think he's surrendering." Francino looked squarely at Burns. "If you want to shoot him, go ahead."

Suddenly, the Japanese soldier sat on the ground. He crossed his legs like a schoolchild and looked warily first at Burns, then at Francino.

"We should get going," said Francino.

"I don't like this," Burns said. "There's something wrong here. No Jap walks out of the jungle and surrenders. What makes you think that he's alone?"

Francino nodded almost imperceptibly.

They'd been waiting for an ambush ever since. Burns was convinced and then not convinced that the Japs were following them with the intention of eating them. Cannibalism, said Burns, was commonplace in Japanese society. Ever since the start of the war, the Japs had supplemented their diet with Allied flesh. That's why, when you killed a Jap and checked his rations, there were only rice balls, no meat. They didn't need to carry it, you see. They liked it fresh. Francino was of the opinion that starving troops didn't carry any rations at all.

"Who told you about the Japs eating people?"

Burns licked his lips. "Jimenez. He lost his best buddy." Burns sensed protest. "Yes he did. Yes he did."

"All right. What happened?"

"It's like what happened to us, only different. I think there were a couple of other guys. Yeah, there were four of them, got cut off, then outnumbered. The Japs didn't kill anyone. They tied them up."

"Did they get the pot boiling?"

"No," said Burns. He looked over at the prisoner. "I swear, that fucking Nip is listening."

Francino shook his head questioningly.

"He is." Burns squinted in suspicion and the prisoner grew deeply solemn.

"They didn't kill anyone . . ."

"Not one," said Burns. "Then they took out the knife."

"Yeah?"

"They cut strips off the guy's leg while he was still alive. Something terrible, that. He was screaming and screaming. They was just carving the steaks right off the guy's thigh."

"What was his name?" asked Francino.

"I told you that. Jimenez."

"Not Jimenez. The guy who was getting carved into steaks."

"I don't know. I think his name was Velasquez."

"Velasquez?"

"Well, he's dead, so who cares?" Burns lifted his two meaty hands to an uncaring God. He left the hands hovering in the air between him and Francino.

"Why didn't they kill him? Why didn't they kill Velasquez?"

"So he wouldn't go bad. They kept him alive so he wouldn't rot."

Francino listened to the sound of his own breath and calmed himself. Even as a story, this was horrifying. Even as a superstition, it was a terrible thing to fear.

Francino was still trying to figure out why the prisoner had delivered himself into their custody. Burns was right. The very act of surrender was not Japanese. He also found the man's silence suspicious. He never protested anything, or attempted any kind of communication. He never insisted in Japanese or responded in any way to their questions. His very ease in their company added to Francino's suspicion. Why was the prisoner calm, resigned? Francino studied him as he marched ahead.

Burns came up close behind Francino. "I've seen you looking at him," he whispered. "You feel it too."

Francino stopped. He looked at Burns's worried face. "Why are you whispering?" he said.

"You know why," said Burns. He tilted his head, swinging his eyebrows in the direction of the prisoner.

Francino shrugged and began walking.

Burns was offended. "Francino, listen to me. Francino."

Francino stopped. He looked at Burns over his shoulder.

"We're on the same side, you dumb Wop. You're no better than me." Burns lifted his shoulders and set his jaw. "Fuck, I even saved your life."

"What is your problem?" said Francino. "You've been gunning for me ever since I got here." He regarded Burns carefully. "Is it just me, or is it all Italians?"

"It might just be you," said Burns. "Or it might just be Italians."

"I'm not going to get drawn into an argument with you," said Francino.

"Cut your losses."

The Japanese prisoner coughed again, and Burns and Francino fell silent. Francino nodded at him and raised his eyebrows to Burns. Burns shrugged his shoulders.

They marched the next hour in tense, silent agreement.

Burns seemed to be struggling with something. Francino had seen it in his frowning, his frequent looks back at him, even though Francino had ignored all of his stares. He didn't want to invite him over, but Burns was determined. He came in close to Francino and shook his head heavily, to make it unmistakable that something was really bothering him.

"You ain't done nothing," he said.

"What?"

"We can't be falling apart like this."

Burns's voice was barely past a whisper and Francino had to listen carefully. He wanted Burns to stop talking. He'd enjoyed the hour of estrangement, which in his opinion was preferable to a reconciliation.

"Italians have good food," Burns said. "Nice-looking women."

"Why don't you just shut up?" said Francino. He marched quickly ahead with the pretense of checking on the state of the prisoner. "Let's stop."

The prisoner fixed his sad, waning eyes on Francino and to Francino's surprise, shook his head. "Do the Japs shake their heads?"

"What?"

"Do they shake their heads?" Francino demanded.

"What do you think I am? The Jap ambassador?" Burns looked almost wounded. The past four days of marching had made him sensitive and moody.

Francino took a sip from his canteen. "So why do you hate Italians?" he asked, resigned.

"Well, a lot of Italians I just don't like," said Burns. He seemed to be relieved of a great weight. "There's only one I hate."

Burns waited expectantly.

Francino took a deep breath. "Mussolini?"

"No," said Burns. From the look on his face, he didn't seem to know who Mussolini was. "DiMaggio."

"Joe DiMaggio?"

Burns nodded solemnly.

"No one hates Joe DiMaggio. Joltin' Joe. The Yankee Clipper. Fifty-six-consecutive-game batting streak. MVP in '41."

"MVP, with a batting average of .357. When Ted Williams—"

"Ted Williams?"

"Ted Williams batted .406."

Francino was silenced.

"If it wasn't for all the songs and the radio coverage—what does that have to do with the game? If the guy's so fucking graceful, give him a tutu."

Francino was too shocked to laugh. Burns was nodding again, maybe to his patron saint or whoever it was who seemed to agree with him wherever he went, whatever generous spirit kept Burns feeling justified. It was because of this—the incomprehension on his part—that Francino didn't realize that the prisoner had stood up and was walking toward them. The prisoner stopped just short of the end of Burns's rifle, which was now readied, and said, "You an idiot." The prisoner was shaking with emotion and his hatred of Burns showed clearly in the spite and accuracy of his words. "Joe DiMaggio is the greatest player, even Ted Williams say that."

Francino took strong steps backward. The shock of hearing the prisoner's fluent English had scared him more than if a knife or gun barrel had been pointed at his face. Burns shoved his rifle at the man's head. The prisoner pushed the gun away with the back of his hand. He had stared death solidly in the eyes and knew he had lost, that dying was just a matter of time. He would have his words first. He would have them, if it was his final act.

"You moron," he said to Burns. "You worried about Japanese eating you? Whole jungle full of fucking cannibal. Not one Japanese. All native from New Guinea eat people. They everywhere."

Burns looked around, frightened.

"You not see them," the man continued. "They like tree, belong here, not stand out like you, like me. You not see them," he repeated.

"He's lying," said Burns.

"Why would he be lying?" asked Francino. "Are you lying?"

"You fucking stupid American! Where you think all the native go? You think they go on vacation—hey, crazy Jap and stinking American shoot each other, why not we go to Palm Spring?"

Francino and Burns hazarded a look at each other.

"Fuck you. Fuck you. Fuck you," said the Japanese soldier. "Fuck all America and all American mother." Then he sat down on the ground as if speaking had been too much, too exhausting.

"Where'd you learn to speak English?" asked Francino.

"University of Michigan," said the soldier, not raising his head. "I have Ph.D. in chemistry."

The prisoner looked upward, where a beam of light projected solidly into the thick air, substantive and menacing. Dead leaves circled through it and slowly wound back to the jungle floor. The light, from where Francino stood, seemed to dissolve into a misty cloud around the prisoner's head. Francino felt a profound, general sadness.

Francino patted himself down and found the cigarette he had been saving for later. He'd liked the idea that he believed in a later. He had a lighter, which had been useful the last few days. Francino walked over to the Japanese soldier and squatted down.

"What the fuck you doing?" asked Burns.

Francino raised his head to Burns. He was surprised. He couldn't speak. His voice stuck in his throat and his eyes felt the unfamiliar sting of tears. He took a deep breath to compose himself. "This man is dying," said Francino, "and I am giving him a cigarette. Do you have a problem with that?"

Burns squinted, then looked away up at the canopy of sky.

"Thank you," said the Japanese soldier. "I shit blood, die soon. I alone."

Francino smiled and lit the cigarette.

"They both born in California," said the Japanese.

"Who's born in California?"

"Williams," said the soldier, "and DiMaggio."

GUINEA · 71

The prisoner fell asleep. Burns was affable, which was all right with Francino, even though he was unsure how to proceed. Francino took his glasses and folded them. He put them in his pocket. They'd been sliding down his nose for days and now seemed pointless.

"Can you see?" asked Burns.

"Yeah," said Francino. "The far stuff is still pretty clear, but I have a hard time making out what's right in front of me."

Burns nodded sympathetically. "You like Australia?"

"Yeah, I like it."

"I'm thinking of relocating after the war. I'd like to maybe get a house in Brisbane."

"Brisbane." Francino smiled. "I won a dance contest in Brisbane," he said. "I was jitterbugging" — here he laughed, because the idea of doing something like that seemed incomprehensible — "with an Australian lady. We were great. After we won, she liked me even more." Francino smiled. "So we kept dancing."

"Dancing?" said Burns.

"Yeah. Dancing. She was nice. She had a nice smell, some kind of perfume. We were getting along and then right in the middle of this dance, my Saint Christopher medal goes flying off my neck."

"Your medal just flew off?"

"Flew right off."

"Must have been some dance."

"Yeah, it was. But get this. She sees the medal and she says, 'You're a Mick and I don't dance with Micks.'"

"You?"

"That's what I say. 'I ain't no Mick.'" Francino and Burns chuckled together. "And she says, 'You're a Catholic. That makes you a Mick. And I don't dance with Micks.'"

When Burns had nodded off and Francino was left to swatting mosquitoes and watching their immobile prisoner, his mind wandered back to Brisbane. There had been a trainload full of

Italian POWs, Axis soldiers. They were all shoved in together in a boxcar like livestock. The boxcar was uncovered and the sun beat down on them. Francino was entranced. He listened to the heavy, sonorous conversations. He understood every word. He looked street-end to street-end and saw two Aussies, one with a broad-brimmed khaki hat, the other darker skinned and hatless, squinting out at nothing—as Aussies were inclined to do—with his hand resting on a street sign and the arch of his left foot set solidly against his right knee. In the boxcar, the Italians were talking about food and drink. Francino fought a desire to join them, climb into their small, familiar prison, to embrace them all and tell them about his family. He patted down his jacket. He had three packs of cigarettes with him. He opened each pack and jumped on a nearby bench. Joyfully, he threw the cigarettes into the boxcar. They snowed down on the prisoners and soon cheers rose out of the car. Francino threw in a box of matches and the Italians roared in approval. Francino almost couldn't hear the Aussies yelling at him, running from all sides to see the why of the commotion. He heard them yelling "Wop," "Neapolitan nigger," and other things, but he didn't care. He was happy for the first time in months.

Francino fell asleep while thinking of this, the boxcar, the Italians he'd met in Australia of all places. His head fell to his chest and his rifle slid to the jungle floor.

He woke to Burns's yelling.

"Fuck, fuck, fuck!"

"What?"

"That fucking Yankee-loving Nip's escaped."

Francino raised his hand in a silencing gesture; Burns's aspect shifted from anger to panic. Francino knew Burns by now and his mind followed the same route. The prisoner had taken off, met up with some Japs. They were in danger. Only Burns had added fear of cannibalism to the equation.

"I ain't gonna let no Nip do that to me," he whispered.

They were in a small clearing at the foot of a large tree. Burns inspected the edge of the greening and discerned some trampled leaves that weren't the work of the previous day's march. He gestured over to Francino, who followed him at a short distance. The sun was pushing through the tall foliate ceiling in blades and Francino, with his eyes partially closed and his breathing quiet, felt the great beast shift beneath him. Burns sighed loudly, sidestepped, and Francino saw the prone, still body of the Japanese prisoner lying unmolested on the jungle floor. The soles of his sandals were bared and one arm reached out ahead, as though he had never given up reaching his destination.

"Japs are like dogs that way," whispered Burns. He turned and looked up at the sky with his rifle butt resting on the jungle floor and his left thumb slung through a belt loop.

Francino dropped to one knee. He rolled the man over. Grubs were making quick work of the corpse and had already invaded the soft membranes of the mouth.

The rain started in the early afternoon. It thundered out of the sky in sheets rather than drops. Keeping upright in the mud and uneven terrain was difficult. Francino was menaced with thoughts of his flesh sloughing off his bones while he was still alive. In the late morning, he'd slipped in some mud and shot down twenty feet into a ravine. It had taken him an hour and a half and all his energy to make it back up the ridge. Then the rain had tapered off. The extreme heat had turned the jungle into a sauna.

"Where are we going?" Francino asked Burns.

"West."

"I thought we were heading south."

"South? It's too steep. And with the rain."

Because it was raining again, a steady patter that occasionally swelled to a deafening drum. His boots sank down to the ankles in mud. More than once he stopped, unwilling to move, until Burns halted and got him back in motion.

The earth shifted once more. Francino looked to Burns. He had not noticed it, nor would Francino tell him, that the great alligator that was Guinea was slowly waking. Her head swung low from right to left and a great claw made the first step forward. Her body moved slowly in a heavy S-shaped tread. Soon, Francino thought, soon he would be dead.

"I thought I could survive this," Francino said. He whispered to himself, half expecting a response, despite the fact he was praying.

"I thought I would live to guide men," he said.

"I am not even half a man," he said.

"I have lost God. I will never find my way home," he said.

He saw a familiar purple cloud hovering above.

Francino knew that he was at the edge of life. Burns pushed through vines and undergrowth, trampling everything, occasionally raising his thick head to smell the air. Francino trailed him desperately, tracked him up the muddy slopes, followed his retreating figure through the walls of mist and vine partitions. While scrambling under the branches of a tree that was growing almost horizontally, Francino caught his neck. He realized that his medallion was hooked and the chain was choking him. Francino yelled for Burns to stop, but Burns did not hear because the rain was falling in torrents. Rivulets in an impromptu waterway coursed past Francino's knees, forking around saplings, knitting back together into a broad, fist-width river. A measured snap of twigs and the crush of greenery advanced slowly as if a snake were approaching him along a low branch. Francino pulled gently at the chain, but it did not come loose. He then gave one solid tug. The chain snapped and for one brief instant he saw the glint of metal—a spark—then all was lost in the deluge.

Francino scuttled up and blindly forged his way in the direction he'd last seen Burns. He called and listened, but all he could hear was the endless rush of water. At the edge of his vision there seemed to be a brightening, a translucence to the vegetation. Francino slipped again, his knee hitting a rock. A sharper pain beside the dull thud of bruising let him know he'd cut himself clear to the bone. He raised his body up from the mud, holding on to a low branch, and limped the last twenty feet.

The vegetation abruptly stopped. Here, there was nothing but air.

Again the rain broke and a blinding sun struck Francino, instantly warming his skin through his heavy, wet clothing. There was a strong wind and Burns, standing a mere ten feet away, was beckoning to him. Francino walked to him only vaguely aware of the pain in his leg. Burns scuttled onto a large boulder that was set into the side of the mountain. Francino climbed after him, helped by Burns's sturdy hands. They had reached the edge of the world.

The earth fell at a steep incline, leaving Francino reeling in the thin mountain air. They had walked out of the jungle not by escaping on the south or west perimeter, but rather had somehow climbed through its ceiling and now stood above it. The air was clean and cool. On all sides, brilliant green slopes fell sharply downward and wisps of clouds caught on the peaks across the valley; farther down, Francino sighted a flat, metallic shimmer that had to be the ocean.

"Well, look at that," said Burns. "Where the fuck are we?"

Francino dropped to a squat. "What does it look like?"

But Francino's words caught in his throat. A sound was floating up from the sea. At first he thought he was hallucinating, but the music wasn't pretty enough to be imagined. He put his hands to his temples and listened. "What is that?"

"That," said Burns, "if I am not mistaken, is 'Scotland the Brave.'"

Francino smiled and listened. It was pipes, bagpipes, and their profound belching and bellyaching echoed and bounced along the valley from the depths of the mud to the steep peaks. Here at the edge of creation the earth sang. Francino sat down. The rock pushed beneath him and he smiled, listening to the gentle groan of the great alligator as she settled back to sleep.

Walkabout

Bob spent most of his life working in Thailand. He was a quiet man who didn't bother with conversation, which didn't bother his coworkers, since Bob didn't seem the type that would make good company. For one thing, he was at least twenty years older than most of the guys who went to the East to work on government-funded projects. For another, he had lost all ties to Australia—including football, cricket, and politics—and didn't return for the expected visits, instead choosing to sign up for one long-term project after another. At first, his colleagues made up stories about him: he had killed his wife; Bob Cairns was not his real name; he was part aborigine, which explained his voluntary solitude. Eventually, the stories died because Bob refused even the smallest donations of corroboration or denial, and the interest in him died with them. Bob kept to himself, and that was all there was to it.

The only thing that Ned knew for sure about Bob was that he was dead. He wasn't even sure what day it happened, as the event had announced itself through a foul odor—the odor of an active and living decomposition—that was winding its way through the laundry chutes and fire escapes of the hotel. Ned was standing in the hallway wrapped in a towel. He had just given his date —the best that Thailand had to offer—a big tip, and was feeling altruistic, a false feeling that often gripped him in a hangover, when he saw the hotel manager, Gary (which the manager pronounced Gah-lee), disappearing around a corner.

"Gary," Ned called. The man stopped in his tracks. He turned around, bobbing his head up and down in greeting, and slowly scuttled back up the hallway. "What's that awful smell?" Ned asked.

"I do not know," said Gary. "You must help me." The manager extended his fine, small hands in front of him. "It is coming from the room of your friend."

"Whose room is it?"

"The other Australian. The old man." Gary bobbed his head up and down. "I am worried . . . He hasn't been to breakfast the last two days. He isn't a late riser like you, Mr. Ned."

Bob Cairns, the sheep and goat expert, had arrived a few days before. Ned had been working on the management end of the project, a lot of noodle lunches with local politicians, and hadn't even had a chance to sit down with him; he'd seen Bob in the lobby—thin gray hair that stood up like a wheat field. Ned pulled on a pair of jeans, then walked barefooted and barechested down the hallway. Gary turned the key slowly in the lock. A cockroach crawled out from beneath the door, waving anxious antennae. The smell was atrocious. Ned stepped back from the doorway. He leaned on the wall gazing at the yellowed wallpaper as the floral pattern danced out of the dusty background. He didn't need to look. He had broken into a sweat. Gary looked up at him, imploringly.

"Poor old bugger," said Ned. "I guess his ticker went."

Bob's journey ended in Pataya on an inauspicious Australia Day bathed in brilliant sunshine. Ned and his friend Gavin had rented a boat—the *Angel II*—some fishing poles, and a wiry Thai named Korn, who was Gary's brother-in-law. The beer was protected in a bucket of ice with a wet towel thrown over it; Ned and Gavin had already put a serious dent in the supply and were feeling merry, even though the topic of conversation was Bob.

"Not a bloody thing. No next of kin. All they had was some defunct address in Western Australia. So I had him cremated. It was the least I could do," said Ned.

Gavin popped open another beer. "Then you drove around with him in the boot of your car for half a year?"

"What was I supposed to do?" Ned looked out at the waves. Ned had been waiting for some sort of instructions from the company—what was he supposed to do with Bob's ashes?—but no one seemed willing to take on the responsibility. At first Ned found driving around with Bob Cairns darkly amusing. He started making conversation, as if Bob were in the passenger seat, rather than bouncing around in the boot of his car with the tool box and spare tire. One night, Ned took the urn with him into the Blue Jeans Bar in Bangkok and told the fellows that Bob Cairns had finally decided to come out for a drink. But recently Ned had heard whispering coming over the back seat, harsh echoes usually in the dead of night, and although he'd clocked this phenomenon up to a combination of ephedrine and Mekong whisky, Ned had decided that it was time for Bob to go. Australia Day was as good as any. Besides, his girlfriend back home had told him that you scattered ashes across the sea. This was the right thing to do.

Ned held the railing of the boat and watched a parasailing tourist being dragged across the sky. Ned thought he was probably German, like most of the tourists, and noted the helium balloon-shaped shadow that he cast on the water. "Beautiful day. Clear sky, all except for Herr Tourist up there."

Gavin laughed. "Well, then, let's do it. All the fish will be off for happy hour if we don't get a move on."

Ned unzipped his duffel bag and took out the urn. "Bob, Gavin. Gavin, Bob."

"I knew Bob," said Gavin.

"Then why didn't you say so?"

"Never met him," said Gavin. "In 1985 we were here in Pataya for the Year of Clean Water conference at the Hilton. Bob gave some talk on livestock management and water contamination. Couldn't have been that long before he died. Anyway, I saw him taking a bathe not too far from here. It was early, maybe six. I was stumbling down the beach coming back from . . . well, that doesn't matter. He wasn't swimming, didn't go into the water beyond his waist, just seemed to walk about at that level. I sat down to have a smoke. He finished, came back up the beach for his towel, and then I saw his legs. They looked like they'd been attacked by a shark or something. There were these huge, round scars, whole chunks of flesh gone. I've never seen anything like it. Those legs could have told a story."

"So could Bob, if he'd wanted to, but he didn't."

Ned unscrewed the cover of the urn and Gavin opened the bottle of Swan Lager, which was to follow Bob into the sea. Bob was from Western Australia and, although Ned and Gavin knew nothing else, they felt sure that Bob had downed some Swans in his time.

"What if he was religious?" asked Ned.

"What if he wasn't?" Gavin looked at the urn and sniffed its contents. "Hell, he's been in God's hands for a while now."

"God's hands," said Ned, "and my boot."

"I can sing something," said Gavin. "I'll sing him a sheep song. 'The Drover's Dream.'"

Ned nodded in approval. Gavin cleared his throat and started in on the song, in a surprisingly lovely voice.

"One night while traveling sheep, me companions lay asleep,
'Twas not a star to 'luminate the sky.
I was dreamin' I suppose, for my eyes were nearly closed,

When a very strange procession passed me by.
First there came a kangaroo, with his swag of blankets blue.
A dingo ran beside him as his mate.
They were traveling mighty fast, but they shouted as they
*   passed,*
You'll have to jog along, it's getting late."

Gavin sang on about the dreaming man, the singing crows and dancing koalas, flute-playing bandicoots and smiling lizards, and how the drover awoke only to find himself beneath his cart, confused and unconvinced that it had all been a dream.

Bob's ashes were stroked across the waves, sucked into the sea's mouth, spat out on the surface. They etched stories where no one would see them and read their traces. The body was no longer. Once, Bob had struggled against it. He'd thought, This body's going to starve and then stop and I'll go along with it, so I better take care of it, 'cause what's the point in going on without a body? And as he heard the monkeys screaming in the canopy of the jungle growth he thought that if he let his body quit that's all he'd be, a monkey's scream. After that, when he heard the monkeys call to one another, he thought that it was Sean, or Paul, or his brother Mark reminding him that they were freed from their corpses but still trapped along the railroad.

Hard to piece it all together, that time. Three years spent that somehow wound themselves into one long second. How long had Mark managed to survive? It was hard to tell. They had been captured together in Indonesia, some distant place where the enemy was still a Japanese soldier and not starvation, where one shouldered a rifle and not a shovel. They made the journey in the hull of the boat, surrounded by pounding waves and dying of thirst. Stopover in Burma. Destination Thailand. Mark had been strong then. He was down from his usual 190 pounds, but was still large and imposing. Bob had always been wiry and, as Mark was whittled away until he weighed only 126, Bob seemed little changed in comparison.

How can you understand the greater purpose of your labor when all you can see is one tiny portion? Bob thought of the Egyptian slaves dragging blocks of stone. Did they even know what a pyramid was or why they were building it? He didn't know. Railroad tracks in the middle of nowhere going to the end of the earth, ties laid in the jungle — men falling dead of exhaustion and lack of food. Sometimes Bob would imagine, as he shoveled, that beneath the tons of mud there'd be a door. The door would lead to his mother's kitchen — no people, just the kitchen — and a steak would be frying heartily on the stove.

The Japanese saw that Bob's brother was an ox during the first week of construction. Four Americans or seven Dutch to one Aussie worker, they said, and Mark was equal to two of his countrymen. Even with dysentery and the first signs of beriberi Mark labored on the railroad, that magical artery, which they had learned would link Bangkok to Burma and eventually India. The railroad meant victory for the Japanese; the POWs were an expendable resource, a lucky find to achieve this end. Side by side, Bob and his brother shoveled the endless mud toward an Allied defeat. Often they were waist deep in fetid water, careful not to go in any deeper, if it was possible. That was what the Dutch doctor said. His English wasn't good enough to explain why at first, but he would learn the word "cholera."

The mind slipped as the body labored. Bob's thoughts twisted and soared, escaping the pain of his overtaxed muscles. Once, while his mind had been flying around, he had fallen to the ground beneath a blow delivered by a guard. Bob wasn't sure what his body had done to inspire this, and he really didn't care. He thought he'd stay lying there. Maybe he'd just die like that, and that would be better. Maybe death would offer a moment's peace, but something rebelled, something he could not understand, and he'd forced himself up and back to work. Some strange spirit inhabiting Bob's body wanted to live.

Or maybe it was just Mark whispering as he shoveled, "You'll be right," that raised Bob to his feet. Bob thought about the sheep-shearing competitions back home, which Mark always won. The other shearers said it wasn't fair. Smiling, they said that Mark hypnotized the sheep. He would pull one from the pen, flip it on its back, and whisper to it, "You'll be right." The sheep would lie still then, beneath the clippers. In a few seconds, expertly shorn with barely a nick, they'd leave his reassuring hold.

The art of hypnotizing sheep. This was serious business, as far as Bob was concerned, but Paul and Sean, who were city boys from Perth, didn't understand. They had a joke about it. "Mark's hypnotized that Korean guard," they said. "Mark's got him eating out of his hand." The guard did like Mark, although he was careful that the Japanese officers didn't notice. His respect for the great Australian expressed itself in extra helpings of rice and the occasional egg that made it into Mark's dinner. "He treats you like the prize ram," Bob whispered to his brother. "Be careful. You know what prize rams are used for." And Mark had nodded, laughing at his brother's concern. "Breeding stock," Mark said.

The Korean guard shot himself one evening, wasted one of the emperor's bullets into his skull. The guard had visited Bob, who was down with wet beriberi, right before he did it. Bob's body was distended and bulging with fluid; his testicles were as large as grapefruit. He was surprised when the Korean guard came into the hut that served as an infirmary. The guard's hair stood straight up, but Bob could not remember if it always did that, or if his shock of black hair just looked frightening now that the man seemed so disturbed. Bob saw an unnatural sweat on his brow and noted the way he moved—crazed and afraid—like a sheep with magnesium deficiency. The Korean touched Bob's shoulder, which was a strange and disquieting gesture. "Same, same, prison-uh," he said, motioning in a way that made it clear that as far as he was concerned, Koreans and Australians were in a similar position. Then he left. Shortly after that, Paul came in. "Are you in for that ulcer?" Bob had asked. Paul shook his head and glanced at the pussing hole on his leg. He produced a cigarette, which was a minor miracle, and a stick with a glowing ember to light it with. Bob took the cigarette. Paul had been sent out on the same work detail as Mark, and Bob knew immediately. Paul said, "I fell down. Mark was helping me up and someone saw. That Korean guard . . ." The guard had been ordered to smash in Mark's head with the flat back of a shovel. Then they heard the gunshot ring out and the monkeys screamed.

Bob survived the beriberi. The Dutch doctor had scrounged some rice husks from an abandoned village and made biscuits with them, which were a source of vitamin B. He decided the reason he'd survived was to carry back Mark's spirit and that was enough. In his mind he heard Mark's mantra often: "You'll be right. You'll be right." Then he'd look to the jungle ceiling, not sure of what he'd see, conscious of Mark's spirit trapped like a mosquito in the net of vines. Bob was convinced that Mark was still watching over him, as he'd always done. Sometimes, he'd hear his brother's voice. "Christ, Bob, take care of yourself. Those ulcers'll kill you." And Bob would whistle up at the leafy sky the first bar of "The Drover's Dream," and Mark would finish off the line.

Bob left his battle against beriberi, and starvation once more became his number-one adversary. He remembered Mark sitting high on his horse, his face set in grim determination. Life had not been easy on the station those prewar years.

"The whole fucking country's gone broke," Mark had said, shaking his head.

Bob mounted his horse and trotted up beside him. "Which ones do we shoot?" he asked.

Mark held the rifle in his lap, looking down on it in a pained way. "We shoot the ones that aren't gonna make it." The slaughter was to ensure that some had food, but killing one's own flock was not easy; the sheep were their life blood—Australia rides on the sheep's back, people said—and this was poor gratitude.

Sean turned to Bob, who was still on the station shooting sheep, and said, "Do you know the Yanks gamble their rice?"

"What?"

"The Yanks, they gamble their rice."

"What if you keep losing?"

Sean nodded in an emphatic, disgusted way. "They let each other starve. They con each other out of life."

Bob thought about this for a minute. "Sometimes, the weak make way for the strong," he whispered, but Sean did not hear. He was too involved sharpening a spoon edge—which was the only surgical instrument in camp—for the doctor. Sean went on to talk about the Poms and their divine right, the Dutch and their cowardice, worked his way up to the Korean guards, and then the Japanese themselves. But Bob knew that among all of these, the real enemy was time and the real war was between its passage and one's body.

"Take care in the not breaking of the skin," the Dutch doctor said. "Infection likes it. That is why the tropical ulcer." Easier said than done. Down the river, the Aussie doctor lopped off the limbs infected with the deep pussing wounds, legs mostly. But the Dutch guy, he knew better. On the railroad, they had marines in place of anesthesia. Four marines, one for each limb, and a good friend to hold one's head. And the spoon nicely sharpened to scoop away the dead flesh, which ate the living. And now Bob, ready for surgery, lying flat on his back pinned down, Paul at his head the way Bob had been for him before. Bob had seen this done many times and his fear was that of one who knew. He could not scream loud enough. Men died hiding their ulcers, more fearful of the cure than of the disease. He was not one of these. His scream rang out. His life held on in the mud and terror and could not escape. When the marines finally released him and he looked into the doctor's eyes, which were calm and sympathetic, he thought that little had been done to save him. The truly dead flesh was within, hidden beneath the layers of taut skin, tissue, and bones, in a place where the doctor's spoon could not remove it.

Of the three in their group that were left, Paul was the sickliest. His battles with amebic dysentery were bloody and hard fought. Sean watched over him like a mother. He would sit by Paul's bedside, filled with fear and worry.

"You know, Bob, this is all right for us, but not for Paul. He was at the university. He studied physics," Sean said.

"Still doesn't make it right for anyone," said Bob.

"No, listen. He signed up with me because he thought I was too bloody stupid to make it alone."

"What'd he think we'd be doing out here? Solving problems?"

"Oh, I dunno. Paul shouldn't be here."

Which made it seem to Bob as though Sean found the situation tolerable for the rest. Paul took a turn for the worse and was delirious much of the time. Bob found it strange when he entered the hut one evening and found Paul alone, without his usual nurse.

"How're you doing, Paul?" asked Bob.

"Debloodylightful," said Paul. Profanity put Bob's mind at ease. Sean appeared at the door of the hut. At first he revealed himself in silhouette, but after he stepped out of the shadow, Bob saw that Sean's shorts were gone and in their place was a kind of G-string—a loose swatch of cloth that draped around his loins like a diaper.

"Now there's one the midwife should have strangled," said Paul.

Sean was smiling. He made his way over quickly and produced two small bricks wrapped in banana leaves. "One for Paul, and one for Bob and me to split. It's sugar."

"And where are your shorts?" asked Paul.

"Covering some Burmese backside," he replied.

Paul struggled onto one elbow. He looked over at Sean and managed a smile. "Out of gratitude for your generosity, I will recover." And he lived.

Paul looked terrible, sicker than the sick, emaciated to the point that it was almost comic that he wasn't dead. Paul had one tooth left, sticking up from his lower gum like a tombstone. His shorts had rotted off his body and he too, like Sean, was now in a diaper, which showed off every protrusion and hollow. He became the object of envy, since he no longer did hard labor. Rumor had it that the Japanese soldiers were scared of him, that they couldn't figure out which dimension he belonged to; he was a constant memento mori, a specter that wouldn't quit. Paul worked with the doctor when he could, and lay down when he couldn't. Sean was pleased at the state of affairs. He had always been a little simple, but as time progressed, he seemed downright loony. He seemed to think that Paul had left the study of physics in Australia for medical school in Thailand.

Bob continued shoveling ten hours a day, seven days a week. Each day someone died and he found himself scanning the gang's faces in the morning, trying to figure out who it would be. He saw the same searching eyes focus on him. He was now about ninety five pounds and looked downright skeletal. Bob marveled at Paul, wondering how anyone could make him look good. Sixty pounds was missing and where was it? Lost in the mud below the pillars that pressed the railroad into the sky. Lost with the bodies that they'd buried in yesterday's embankment, handy filler when one couldn't place a call to a quarry for stone.

One evening Sean came running up to where Bob and Paul sat. Sean was laughing hysterically and at first Bob thought he'd gone off, like the rice that he was eating.

"Want to hear something really funny?" Sean said.

A couple of months had passed since someone had said that, and Bob and Paul were at a loss as to how to respond.

"Of course you do," said Sean. "Shoulda been on duty for this one, Paul. Your friend the doctor, he's not bad, y'know? Anyway, this Jap guard comes up to him. He's all squirmy, y'know, wriggling around and all that, and he tells old Dutchy that he's caught something from the last round of Korean hookers that passed through here, right? And he wants Dutchy to do something about it. And so Dutchy gives him something, tells him to rub it all over his dick. Next thing you know, the Jap's screaming like a madman, running around like someone lit a fire in his shorts. And we're all surprised, but it's so bloody funny, and we can't laugh 'cause we're scared he'll bash our heads in, right? But the doctor's telling him that it's supposed to feel that way, but we know something's up, y'know? So when he's gone, we go up to Dutchy and we ask him, 'What'd you give him?' and Dutchy says, 'The Japanese soldier should not put the penis where the penis is not wanted.'"

Which was a funny story; Bob knew it. He smiled along with Sean and Paul, but somewhere, along the railroad, he had forgotten how to laugh. Laughter was strange music.

The romusha introduced the inconceivable—that there was a level of hell below the one that Bob haunted. These villagers, Thais and Burmese, understood nothing, labored in ignorance. They died in huge numbers out of seeming confusion, as if they didn't realize that one needed to struggle to survive, as if it didn't occur to them. The Japanese didn't seem to think that the villagers needed food or doctors; they didn't seem to think that the railroad constituted a significant change from village life, and they miscalculated the romusha's ability to survive. The romusha were even more expendable than the whites. In the end they got their revenge. They introduced the only worthy opponent to the Japanese—cholera. Cholera was not racist, nor did it have any respect for rank. Cholera cast its lot with the winners and the losers in equal numbers and won most of the time. It tore through the camp, taking most of the romusha, and as it raced down the river it took Paul and Sean along with it. When there was bamboo for fuel, the cholera dead were burned in huge pyres. Bob helped build these monuments, doused them with gasoline, lit them. As the bodies sizzled and seized they would sit up with mouths open in a silent scream until the flames left nothing. Bob learned quickly to burn the bodies face down.

Paul was one of the first to go. Bob sat up with Sean that night. He listened to him crying, a sound that was answered by the monkeys and night birds. Sean's crying was the most beautiful thing he had ever heard. One week later, Sean was dead. The night he carried Sean to the pyre, as he lay in dreamlike sleeplessness, Bob returned home. He was in the kitchen and Noreen Grey was washing up in his mother's sink.

"Where's your brother?" she asked as her pale, freckled arms dipped into the sudsy water. "He's supposed to take me into town tonight."

Bob had looked down at his hat, which he held in his hands. "He's over at the Carvers' fixing a tractor. He said he'd be a little late."

"A little late? He'll be drunk by the time he gets back here." She shook her head in disbelief.

"Noreen, you don't have to do that."

"And who's going to do it? Your mum? Doesn't she have enough to do around here? I can just see you and Mark in Germany face to face with Hitler. You've got your rifles aimed straight at his head and you're both saying, 'Where's mum? Shouldn't she do this?'"

"We're not going to Germany, Noreen."

"Oh, you'll clean the Japs up in a couple of weeks. Just you see. I've got a mind to go to Indonesia myself. I'd show them."

"Yeah, you would, but then who'd give us hell when we got home?"

Noreen had a temperament to match her red hair; she was a good match for Mark, didn't let him outshine her. Bob remembered Noreen's arms best of all, pale and freckled, strong and slim. Her beautiful, empty arms.

The sky broke open one day, as though a fissure ran along the endless heaving gray, a crack the length of the railroad. The Japanese were not perturbed by the start of the monsoon. The will of the emperor was to be obeyed, even as entire chunks of the mountainside slid into the river, which was already choked with bloated carabao, and huts, and once-buried POWs who found themselves making a hasty postmortem retreat down the Mekhong. Standing in the river, dragging a huge teak pillar, Bob had only peripheral vision. The water poured out of the sky in a steady stream, not a drop to be discerned, registering everything amorphously. The river was full of coconuts. Maybe some unfortunate barge had overturned, but Bob felt lucky. Hidden from the guards by the trunk of the tree, he surreptitiously reached for one of the coconuts, grabbed at it, but all he came up with was a handful of hair bound together by some rotted skin.

Most of the floating heads and the accompanying bodies belonged to the romusha, since many of their dead hadn't been buried in the first place. Bob and Sean had worked together on burial duty (there were too many romusha to burn) for the first part of the cholera epidemic. Then Bob had buried the bodies, working alone. One time, when he was dragging a man toward the pit, face down as was his preference, he was accosted by the recently departed's wife. The woman held a two-year-old girl by the wrist and was madly trying to communicate. She started fluttering her hands in butterfly motions, constantly looking to the jungle ceiling. Bob did not understand. His mind had been full of thoughts of the unfortunately small size of the man's feet and the decent sandals, which were now protecting soles whose contact with dirt would no longer require them. The woman went on and on, then finally wrested her husband's ankles out of Bob's hands and began slowly dragging the man away. Watching her reminded Bob of an ant struggling with a bloated grain of rice.

Later, Bob learned that most of the romusha were of the opinion that if you buried bodies, their souls could not escape.

The first question Bob asked Tom Reilly when he learned that he had a radio was "How old am I?"

"Oh, I dunno. It's July 1944."

"I'm twenty-one." And Mark, wherever he was, was twenty-four. Now the news was that the war was ending. An odd tension filled the camp then. Bob felt consumed with an unfamiliar pain. It took him a while to figure out it was hope. He was hauling a body to the pit for burial, a wet beriberi. Wet beriberis didn't burn. He had the arms of the bloated man and was struggling up a muddy slope when the body burst, drenching him and his companion with the stagnant juices. For a moment he thought he would cry, but it passed. What was he hoping for? The long road that wound its way through the flat bush toward his family home would only bring the war back to a place that he had hoped to protect from it. He would no longer be a person but a reminder of absences—Mark's and his own. He was now an ugly thing, a sore upon the landscape, a battered body which told a story that no one wished to hear.

Bob's survival was incomprehensible. The wedding was an odd affair. Bob's jacket was now too big; he worried that people would think it was Mark's. Noreen wore a dress that she'd ordered during the war to keep her spirits up—something to distract her from Mark's agonizing silence. Her eyes were red around the edges as she walked to stand before the minister. Bob felt like a ghost darkening what should have been a happy event, even though everyone agreed that he was doing the right thing. He stared at the bowls of coleslaw, steaks, and pineapple chicken on the checkered tablecloth in complete noncomprehension; he regarded the cake—fruitcake with plastic icing as demanded by tradition—which looked more like an enameled tooth than anything else. The day was punctuated with uncomfortable silence. Bob and Noreen circled each other in close, awkward orbits, never touching. She smiled bravely and her strength was admirable. No one mentioned Mark, which made it obvious that all were thinking of him. Few people danced to the violin's entreaties; few people sang. As evening settled over the gathering, the beer began to take hold on Bob's father. He rubbed tears from his eyes and he set his mouth in a bitter, clenched way. Bob went to sit across from him—silent and comforting, but his father looked away.

Noreen accepted the situation. She seemed to remember Bob talking more than he did, but wasn't altogether sure. The expanse of red land that stretched in a never-ending flatness had a way of sucking the sounds out of the house. The land swallowed all conversation, and replaced it with a thin film of dust that coated everything—fresh puddings, eyeballs, sheets. Besides, if Bob had a lot to say, he probably wouldn't have the time to say it.

Bob worked long hours riding out to the far corners of the station. Usually he was with Stan, an aborigine, who seldom spoke. Stan had thoughts of his own that he never shared and the two enjoyed a mutual, comfortable silence; they only discussed what was essential—sheep, dogs, and drought. Even during lunch, while Bob sprawled up against a tree and Stan squatted completely still, only moving to swat the flies that crawled near his eyes, they never conversed. Sometimes, Stan would squint hard at the barren landscape and Bob would look, but see nothing but the baked land or an occasional lizard, and Stan would say "dingo" or "rain" or "stray." Although Bob could never see the evidence of what inspired these words, Stan was never wrong. He was more a part of the bush than a part of the sheep business. Even Stan's features echoed the landscape: a flattened nose that flared into nostrils, like the eroded rock protrusions with their mysterious caves; wiry hair, which reminded Bob of the toughest, drought-surviving grass; brilliant white teeth that gleamed as pure and indestructible as polished limestone; limbs as thin and supple as a gum tree. When one day Stan disappeared, Bob was not altogether surprised. Noreen, who was eight months along at the time, thought the situation to be intolerable.

"Noreen, let it go," Bob had said. "There's a guy out at Coonawarra says he's looking for something. I'll drive over there later."

"Where'd Stan go? You've been working with him a whole year and then he just up and leaves?"

Bob just shook his head.

"You're out there twelve bloody hours a day. He must have said something."

"He didn't have to. He's on walkabout, Noreen."

Walkabout. Strange. The black workers did that, one day in the routine and seemingly happy, the next stricken with the need to leave all behind. Sometimes it was over in a matter of days. Sometimes they showed up months later. Or they never came back at all. A few people had a respect for the spiritual aspect, but the majority of the station owners found the walkabout thing damned inconvenient. Noreen returned from the kitchen with a beer. At first Bob thought it was for him, but she drank half the bottle in quick silent gulps. She looked over at Bob with her head cocked to one side.

"This guy over at Coonawarra, is he black?"

Some people claimed that Stan was still in the area. They saw him every now and then, but it was a big area, and at any rate, Stan had done nothing about getting his old job back.

A couple of weeks later, Bob got an invitation in the mail. He looked at the tasteful cream-colored envelope for a good five minutes before he opened it. A reunion was incomprehensible. All those years of longing to see other faces and people who had not been reduced to sinewy specters . . . And now they were talking about renting a banquet room at the Sheraton in Perth. Did Bob want to make a donation? Was he going to bring his wife? He let his hand that still held the letter dangle off the side of the chair. Noreen, who was now enormous, took his wrist and read the letter sideways.

"I'm telling you, Bob, you should go. It'll be good for you."

"Noreen, don't be daft."

"It's time to put the past where it belongs."

"Noreen, I'm warning you. This is none of your business."

"None of my business? Two more weeks and you'll be a father. What then?"

"What does that have to do with—"

"Everything, Bob. It has everything to do with everything."

Bob crumpled up the invitation and sent it flying across the room. He went into the kitchen for a beer. Now that Noreen was very pregnant she could no longer race him for the fridge where she would fling herself in front of it, barring access until she'd had her say. The invitation had been signed by Graham Watt. Bob had no idea who Graham Watt was. Was Graham Watt leading a good life? Were Thailand and the railroad things that Graham Watt wanted to remember?

Bob got insomnia that night. Noreen had learned to sleep through his late-night peregrinations and no longer questioned sleepily from her side of the bed. Bob wandered out the back door—stepping carefully over the dog, who twitched and whined in a dream about a particularly stubborn ewe—onto the back veranda. The sky stretched in an immense blackness across the land and the stars glowed through it fiercely. Bob thought that night was a threadbare cloak pulled across the white heat of day. The darkness was comforting. He looked out in the direction of the shed, where a gentle breeze rattled the corrugated iron in a rhythmic way. Possums shook the branches overhead and the smell of wattle drifted in from the creek. Bob was thinking of walking over to the bottlebrush tree, where he'd seen a wombat earlier that week, when he noticed a figure standing in the gloom. He had his right foot resting against his left knee and was leaning on a stick. Bob watched, his heart pounding, because the stick seemed to resemble the long arm of the shovel. And he, whoever he was, was staring out protectively in the direction of the flock. Bob shuddered, then drew himself up and began to walk in the direction of the man. He was about to call to him, when he realized that he was not supposed to speak. Instead, he whistled the first few notes of "The Drover's Dream." Bob waited for the response, and the wind carried it back to him, mournful and strange. Mark had returned. That was all. Bob turned in silence and headed back to the house. But if he'd listened carefully, he would have recognized that the notes belonged to a magpie heralding the coming day. And if he'd only taken a few more steps, he would have realized that the figure was Stan, lost in meditation of his last night in the area, studying the stars that would dictate his wandering.

The next morning, Bob awoke early with the events of the previous night weighing heavily on him. This cloudy frame of mind was not lifted by the thick black coffee. What was Bob supposed to do now that Mark had returned? Bob heard Noreen stirring in the next room and decided to head out to the feed store before she got out of bed.

Norm Burnside was in town that day. He was carrying a sack of oats and at first it seemed that the bandy legs and battered hat belonged to the sack rather than the man who was struggling along beneath it, but the hat was Norm's. Norm was one of the old fellows who still kept corks bobbing around the brim of the hat, attached by fishing line, to keep the flies out of his eyes. Bob hadn't seen him in years, not since before the war. That was not uncommon in a place where the stations were huge kingdoms unto themselves. You saw your neighbors at shearing time or at the rare social gatherings, which were usually at shearing time anyway. People often limited their sorties into town to a few times a year and running into someone was more of the exception. Norm heaved the sack of oats into the back of his truck and looked over at Bob with the same squinty-eyed expression that he used when tallying up the casualties of the latest drought. Norm didn't recognize him at first; Bob took his hat off to give Norm a good look before they even greeted each other.

"Hello, Bob."

"Good to see you, Norm. How's your wife?"

"She died last week. Wasn't in good health the last few years."

"I'm sorry, Norm. She was a good woman."

"That she was."

They looked down at the dusty street in a moment of respectful silence.

"Terrible about Mark," Norm finally ventured. "Now there was a good lad. Handsome and strong. Best sheep shearer I ever saw . . ."

Bob nodded in agreement.

"Hear you married Noreen Grey . . ."

Bob nodded again. "Is there gonna be a funeral?"

"Funeral? I'm afraid not. It's been too hot . . ."

"Well, it's been good seeing you, Norm. I'll pass the sad news along to my mother. She always liked . . ."

"Margaret."

Bob nodded and returned his hat, lowering the brim across his forehead. He watched Norm's pickup, followed by a cloud of dust, as it edged toward the line of the horizon. Bob looked down the road that led back to his house. Somewhere back there was Mark; he could hear him laughing. The laugh echoed in his head, but Bob could no longer conjure up Mark's features. His face wavered in false memories; his likeness was recalled in the framed photographs that littered mantels all the way to Perth. Mark with a trophy. Mark in uniform. Mark holding a merino in an awkward embrace, shears poised. Mark with his arm around his little brother — two-dimensional memories that seemed far removed from truth. They were not his recollections but the legends of his townspeople.

Bob picked up the sack of feed and put it in the back of his truck. With a red handkerchief, he wiped the sweat from his brow. The sun was still high in the sky. Bob squinted up until the yellow glare bathed all in a cleansing white, erasing the feed store, the road, his truck. He knelt down to his shoelaces and tied them in firm knots. He stood, pulling himself straight until the two tricky joints in his back snapped into alignment, and then he began to walk.

Folly

K ees bouman stood alone in the sala of his house. The breeze, which had earlier bowed the tops of the palms, was suddenly quiet and the only sound was the clock as it shuddered to each tick. Middle age was making him contemplative, he thought, because with each forward step of the clock, second by second into a modern future, Bouman felt the jungle struggle forcefully against it. Here in the tropics there was one endless season that cycled on and on, then circled back onto itself like a serpent eating its tail. He felt like the first, or maybe the last, man on earth. His evening tea was not waiting on the table and his daughter, Katrina, was not ready to serve it.

Bouman went to stand at the door. The orange sun was sinking fast behind the topmost brushes of the palms. There was a soothing *hush hush* of waves, out of sight from where he stood. A bird excited by the final moments of the day let forth a rattling cackle, beat the warm air with its wings, then followed the sinking sun into the jungle. If his wife had still been alive, she would have stood on the doorstep and started yelling. One call from her and the entire household would have leaped to attention, come running across the swept dirt of the compound. The very chickens would have cackled to life. That gnarled pony tied to the post would have raised his head in respectful attention, but Bouman could only transfer his weight from one bare foot to the other, adjust the waist of his baggy pants, and hope that someone would notice him so forlorn and bereft of tea.

He smelled chicken curry. Bouman looked to the cooking shack and was surprised to see Katrina exit. She was wearing her new white kabeya, the one embroidered in a floral motif, which had been very costly; she was hurrying through the compound's center with such speed that she lost her slipper and had to go back for it.

"Katrina!" called Bouman.

She stopped, stunned, and seemingly guilty. "Father?"

"Where is my tea?"

Katrina put her slipper on and turned back in the direction of the cooking shack.

"What is this nonsense?" he called again.

"Father, we have a visitor."

"A visitor?"

"He's on the veranda. I'll bring the tea there."

Bouman raised his eyebrows in resignation. He hadn't heard anyone on the veranda but now on reentering the living room he could hear the low voice of Aya, the housekeeper, chattering away. He peeked out the door and sure enough, seated at the table—on which someone had set a large stinking bunch of frangipani—was a young native in brilliantly pressed colonial whites. Bouman looked at his own bare feet and baggy batik pants with some amusement. His European shirt, made from coarse local cotton, was frayed at the collar. Bouman felt a certain pride in all of this, especially the way that it would annoy Katrina, the way her immaculate dress was annoying him. Aya was squatting on the floor next to the visitor's ankles. Her elbows rested on her knees and she absently swatted the air in front of her face for mosquitoes.

When Aya noticed Bouman she jumped up straight.

"Tea," she said, embarrassed.

"Oh, forget the tea," said Bouman. "Gin now and some limeade for our visitor."

"Mr. Bouman . . ." The visitor was now standing, his hands clasped behind his back, his head at a respectful incline.

"Yes, I am Bouman. And you?"

"I am Tan Lumbantobing. I deeply appreciate your hospitality."

"I can take no credit for that," said Bouman. "But I am not so rude as to deny that the hospitality of my daughter and my housekeeper is correct and admirable." Bouman smiled. He was actually relieved at his guest, better than a European planter, who would be eager for fresh sympathy over disease and sullen workers. "You will not mind if I call you Tan?"

The young man smiled.

"Are you a visitor or a customer?"

"That depends on what you're selling."

"You are looking for weapons and gunpowder." Bouman shook his head. "Excuse my frankness, but I am an old man and don't want to die not having spoken my mind." Bouman was just forty-five, but felt a great deal older. The sun had creased his skin and the army had calcified his joints, which made him seem old at first but, on closer look, permanent.

The drinks arrived and Bouman poured himself a glass of gin. Tan was smiling at his hands in subtle, respectful silence.

"I would offer you gin, but I suspect your religion forbids it. If you care to help yourself, go right ahead."

Tan took the glass of limeade. He sipped and nodded at Bouman. "This is very refreshing," he said.

"Yes," said Bouman, "refreshing. I prefer my beverages steeped and aged—pickled berries," he said, raising the gin, "or dead leaves soaked in hot water."

Katrina appeared at the door with the tea. She set it down on the table and wiped her hands on her skirt. She was flushed and distracted.

"Sit down, for heaven's sake. Have some tea. Have some gin, if you like." Katrina did not move. She looked from the guest, back over to her father, then at her hands. She was paralyzed with embarrassment.

"Where's the food?" said Bouman to his daughter.

"It will be ready soon," Katrina whispered.

Bouman took a mouthful of gin and closed his eyes. He smiled. "She is a quiet girl," he said to Tan, "but good. She is nothing like her mother, who was wild and, in my opinion, better. I find it hard to believe that there was something that could kill that woman, but there was. And now she is dead ten years."

"You are lucky to have a daughter to care for you," said Tan.

"Yes. Yes, I am." Bouman drank again. "And you, where is your family?"

"My father is in Aceh. My brother is also on a buying expedition. He has gone to the west."

"How are you traveling?"

"By prahu."

"I saw none."

"My brother has taken the boat with him. I do not mean to tax your hospitality, but your housekeeper told me that I could stay in a room in the manager's quarters. It is only for one week."

"You are welcome to stay as long as you like." Bouman did not care what Tan did with his time. "You are from Aceh?"

The young man nodded.

"A relative of the raja?"

"Yes."

"I trust he is alive and well?"

"Alive, but not well."

Even better, thought Bouman. "Did he speak of me?"

"Only to say that during the war, you had been on opposite

sides, but if there was one Dutchman in Sumatra who could give me a straight answer, it was you."

"I was on the side of pepper. That's what we fought for in Aceh. Many lives were wasted, uselessly, on both sides. I will not have the stuff on my table."

"Pepper?"

"Pepper and war, so if we must talk of arms, we will do so after we eat." Bouman spun his glass on the table.

"You lost your fingers in Aceh?" asked Tan.

Bouman raised his right hand. The thumb was solid and his fore- and middle fingers had survived the war, but the other two were sheared right off. The shadow of Bouman's altered hand fell across Katrina's face. "During the war, but not because of it. A bull elephant frightened by the conflict entered camp. Some were trampled and in the effort to kill it, a stray bullet took off my fingers."

"I am sorry that you lost your fingers."

"Oh, I still have them, and later, if I've had enough of this stuff" — Bouman raised his glass — "I will show them to you."

Katrina looked shyly at her father. She had an overbite and when she was uncomfortable, struggled to get her mouth closed over her teeth. Despite this, she was pretty. Bouman thought she had taken the best physical traits of her mother, the gentle brow, the broad cheeks, the unblemished skin that glowed in the sun. From him, she had inherited horsy European teeth — at odds with her small jaws — and social awkwardness. At seventeen she looked more womanly than her full-blooded native peers. She also lacked their guile and awareness. Bouman noticed sadly that Tan had taken a few cautious glances in Katrina's direction and that her burning cheeks and anxiety had been noticed and seen as encouragement.

During dinner Katrina cowered behind the floral arrangement. When Tan thought Bouman so involved with his food that he was not being watched, he slid the flowers slightly to the left with the tip of his knife to take a better look at the girl. She was concentrating on her food, taking the tiniest bites. When she saw Tan watching her, she met his eyes frankly and nervously. It was not he who rattled her, it was her father. Bouman ate fast, without conversation, and loudly. To keep up Tan choked down the chicken and bitter squash, which was spicy and good, only clearing his throat with water. The entire meal took ten minutes. Katrina was not even halfway through her food when the men stood up together and went to stand by the railing to smoke, or in the case of Tan, to pinch a little betel nut, as was his custom after dinner.

"I sent her to Batavia for school," said Bouman, smoke pouring out the corners of his mouth. The two men stood now on the edge of the veranda and a bright moon hit the water and the trees, lighting everything with a pleasing, silver glow. "When she chooses to speak, she can speak in Dutch and French." He smiled at his daughter, who had overcome her shyness enough to smile back. "She came back with a taste for embroidered cloth and now wants me to buy her a piano. I can no longer eat with the simple smell of meat. Now I must be menaced at the table by bouquets of these tough, native flowers whose cheap perfume makes the food taste like shampoo."

"Women like pretty things," said Tan. Bouman took in Tan's soulful eyes and long-fingered, elegant hands. His hair had a sheen to it. Bouman laughed.

"And men," he said, "care only for drink, and barring that, war." Here Bouman gazed knowingly at his guest.

"I don't need to darken this evening with business," said Tan. "I am enjoying your hospitality and I can wait until tomorrow."

"Why," said Bouman suddenly, his face gripped in a smile, "why do you think that I have weapons?"

Tan nodded a few times and turned to his host, who was now only inches from his face. "I know that you have supplied hunters with weapons. They have come out of the jungle with elephant, rhinoceros, tiger, boar. They have taken their heads mounted back to Europe. And you have supplied the cartridges to this end."

"No more hunters for me," said Bouman.

Tan was poised to speak, but then changed his mind. He raised his limeade in a quick, silent toast.

"What were you going to say?"

"What do you mean?"

"Be frank with me. It is the only way to get what you want."

"I don't intend to be disrespectful."

"Of course not."

"You are the supervisor of the trading post."

"Ah. And you would like to speak to the owner?"

Both Tan and Bouman looked up the coast, where a mere two hundred feet away there was another house, much like Bouman's, only this one was still and dark. "Peter Versteegh is on a hunt," Bouman said.

"When did he leave?"

"Five years ago."

"When do you expect him back?"

"I don't," said Bouman. "He was foolishly hunting with a stout businessman from Marseille, someone he knew from the trade. They were hunting orangutan. I suspect the Batak got them, that Versteegh's bony head is gracing a chieftain's mantel as is that Frenchman's. He had a very plump head and impressive mustaches. Even I could see the value in collecting a head like that . . ."

"Father!"

"Ah. She speaks. I'm sorry to offend." Bouman laughed. "Go get some sweets for our guest. I'm sure we have something."

Bouman waved Katrina off. She reluctantly pushed away from the table and the chair legs ground loudly across the floor. Bouman saw her look at Tan with complete frustration and Tan smiled back.

"The Frenchman," whispered Bouman as Katrina left, "had little appreciation for life. He shot an ape and brought it in. It was a female, lactating. He'd lost the infant and didn't seem to care. I went out looking for the baby. I went out for hours, all night, with a lantern. Call me sentimental, but I know what it's like when a child loses the mother."

"Do you really think the Batak killed them?"

"You know better than I do their beliefs, that the ancestors come back as animals—elephant, tiger, and orangutan. Even death is not permanent. I saw little value to the lives of Versteegh and this Frenchman. His name, I remember, was Guillotte. Yes. And they are dead."

"But you say they are still hunting?"

"I wrote to Guillotte's family saying that I doubted he would return. And as for Versteegh, his native wife is still living in the house. Why would I write to his cousins in Holland? They would come and sell this and where would I go? And why should they have this place? You cannot put the value of our little house, our compound, and small business into guilders. Besides, is it not a romantic thought that the Dutchman and Frenchman are wandering through the heart of Sumatra chasing an elusive ape who stays always two steps ahead?"

"A pretty myth," said Tan. "You are romantic, from another time. You forget that it is 1922, that the ways of the ancestors, yours and mine, have long been buried with them. I don't mourn that. Change is good."

"Change?" said Bouman sadly. Katrina appeared in the doorway with a plate. She had picked more blossoms and arranged these in with the rice cakes and wafers. "If I could make this evening last indefinitely, I would do it."

The prahu returned six days later. Bouman had convinced Tan that he had no weapons for sale. Bouman had a half-dozen rifles and countless boxes of cartridges, but Tan was unwilling to name his enemy and rampaging bull elephants were no longer the problem they'd been twenty years earlier. Bouman decided to give the boy a good deal on some bolts of cotton. He'd thrown in a few pairs of embroidered slippers for the boy's relatives, offered gin and tobacco, which had not been of interest, and an immense cooking pot (for boiling missionaries, Bouman had joked), which Tan had thought would be useful. Bouman was just coming out of the warehouse when he saw Tan running down the steps of the house. A figure appeared in the doorway immediately afterward, wiping her eyes with the back of her hand. Tan stopped and turned, then he ran back up the stairs and embraced her. In his shock, Bouman wanted to believe that the woman was Aya, who, gnarled as she was, could offer occasional sexual gratification. But no. It was Katrina and a cold chill slowly took over Bouman's heart.

When Tan entered the warehouse Bouman was sitting at his desk. There was a box of ammunition by his feet. A dozen rifles leaned against the wall. Bouman sat at his desk, his face covered by his hands. Tan could see the man trembling and at first thought that he had been moved to tears, but when Bouman lifted his head, his eyes were clearly fired with anger. Bouman stood up.

"You were a guest in my house and you have deceived me."

"My intentions are honorable."

"Who is the judge of that?"

Tan was silent. "You know my family . . ."

"That they are rich, powerful—yes, I know that. And I tell you that you will never have my daughter. Take the guns. Leave. Never come back."

"She wants to go with me."

"What does she know of what she wants? She is seventeen years old." Bouman picked up a rifle and swung it gracefully to point into Tan's face. "I am offering you the gun. You take the muzzle or the trigger."

Tan was silent.

"I will kill you. I have killed dozens of men in my time and not once has my sleep been disturbed."

Bouman watched the prahu round the promontory and thought with a cautious satisfaction that he would never see the boy again. No doubt, Katrina was in tears and would not speak to him for months. His household was in disorder. Aya would be glaring at him from behind the posts of the house, going about her daily tasks with more than the usual menace; she would be spitting in his food. Bouman shook his head. A stiff breeze stirred the water and the palms dipped and swayed. More than the usual monkey chatter was going on overhead. The birds dipped and swooped with unusual urgency. On the ground Bouman saw the ants coursing fervently in streams. There was the burn of electricity in the air. At the edge of the horizon a beam of lightning flared, leaving the margin a menacing dark purple. Bouman sighed deeply, baring his teeth at the world. He knew he was in for trouble.

About many things, Bouman had been wrong. He was wrong to think that his father-love could satisfy his daughter and wrong to think that he would never see Tan again. By the time the young man returned he was no longer a young man and Bouman had seen so many things—more than twenty years had passed—that he questioned every reality. The very nose in the center of his face was up for debate, as far as he was concerned. But as he squatted and smoked in the burned-out square of earth that had once been his house, he somehow knew that the prahu dipping over the edge of the water, rising up like the sun, bore his old acquaintance, Tan. And Bouman thought, in an uncharacteristically mystical way, that his new clairvoyance meant that his life was drawing to a close.

Tan had lost the colonial whites and was now wearing the baggy batik trousers of his people, those and a European shirt of coarse cotton, with a belt of ammunition slung from shoulder to hip. There was silver in with the black, but he looked much the same. Bouman got up and threw his cigarette. He cocked his head to one side. Tan hesitated, stopping twenty feet from where Bouman stood. To his surprise, Bouman laughed.

"I told you not to come back or I would kill you, but it is you who are armed and I have nothing but these two imperfect hands." Bouman splayed his eight fingers up for inspection.

"How can it be," said Tan, "that you have not changed?"

"A mystery," Bouman shrugged. "I am wiser now and so I will ask you to dinner, to have some tea with me, because I now know what an enemy looks like." Bouman laughed again.

"I thought you were dead," said Tan. "I myself looked in all the nine camps of Sumatra. I had my people check every Javanese camp, every Dutchman."

"Did you not think I might be lost under a different name? And the islands are full of Dutchmen."

"Eight-fingered Dutchmen?" said Tan.

"So thinking I was dead, you came back for my daughter, but it is she who is dead."

Tan was silent.

"That saddens you."

"The Japanese killed many."

"Many, but not her. I have you to blame for that."

"Me?"

"Katrina died in childbirth." Bouman closed his eyes. He heard again Katrina's frightened screams. He remembered Aya's desperate butchery. "Come. Have tea." The Dutchman gestured for Tan to follow. "You can send me back to Holland after dinner."

Bouman had moved into the manager's small house. He walked quickly and Tan followed, two steps behind, his hands resting nervously on his ammunition belt and gun. The sloping thatch roof was repaired with ragged sheets of tin, probably the work of Bouman. He no longer seemed to have anyone in his employ, not even Aya, who would have made her presence known had she been there. Leaning up against a tree to the right of the hut was an ornate, carved door, blunted and polished by exposure. Tan recognized the door as belonging to the original house and wondered what had inspired Bouman to move it from the flames that had no doubt engulfed and destroyed all of his former dwelling. The hut backed onto a wall of vegetation—a development of the last twenty years—and was shadowed and dreary. A few tough vines had lassoed the roof and beams, and soon the hut would be dragged back into the jungle.

Bouman cooked now. He could offer Tan a weak chicken and vegetable broth. Tan set his gun down and took a stool at the table. The sun was low and forced its way inside in blades of harsh light. Soon they would need to light candles. Bouman lit a flame beneath the pot and stirred the chicken. He was whispering to himself, almost singing to the soup. Tan looked cautiously around. There was a hammock in the corner and a sleeping mat rolled up, leaning against the wall. A case of gin (or what had once been a case of gin) acted as a side table and set on that was a greasy candle and, of all things, a Bible. There was a large wooden box on the floor, blackened by the fire, and it took Tan some moments to realize that it had once been a clock.

"You see, I have survived the war," said Bouman, setting the soup before his guest, "but only in pieces."

"Where were you?" said Tan.

"Here."

"Here? The whole war here? Mr. Bouman, how can that be? All the Dutch were transported."

"But the French were not. Remember, Vichy is an ally of the Golden Prosperity Sphere." Bouman smiled slyly, then, reaching behind him to a splintered shelf, he found a passport. He handed it to Tan.

Tan opened the passport. There was Bouman's picture—an old picture, to be sure, where Bouman's fine blond hair actually reached his forehead in a bank rather than one sharp point in the center—the name *Jean Guillotte,* and the birthplace, *Marseille, République de France.*

"Very clever," said Tan. "And how did you survive the natives?"

"I hear a trader down the coast was buried alive," said Bouman with a smile. "But I am lucky. So much sadness puts people off," he said. "They say the ghost of Katrina wanders here, that she will steal your heart as her heart was stolen."

Just then a shadow passed by the window and Tan thought he'd seen her, Katrina, although thinner and darker. He turned quickly to Bouman.

"And you," said Bouman, "do you think Katrina still walks here?"

There was an awkward moment of silence, then a figure appeared in the door, a young woman carrying an infant strapped across her in a batik sling.

"This is Karen," said Bouman.

Tan stiffened. The young woman looked Tan up and down, then turned to Bouman who gave an almost imperceptible nod. This woman was nothing like the shy Katrina. She was darker and Tan realized with a shock that this was his genetic donation. Her eyes met his boldly and it seemed that she recognized him for who he was. Her hair was not brushed but matted into one huge knot at the nape of her neck. Tan calculated that she must be twenty-three years old, but she looked a good deal older. This Karen squatted by the table. She did not seem to care that there was a visitor, but looked at her father with some slyness and satisfaction.

Tan had anticipated another situation altogether, where he was in charge, but now Bouman and the woman were grinning at each other across the table in an exclusive way that could easily be taken as clairvoyant. No, thought Tan, madness. He took a spoonful of soup and began planning his departure.

The soup was odd, slightly bitter, with a nutty aroma that he could not place. People ate many strange things during the war and in the deprivation following. Tan wondered if perhaps the soup had been flavored with wood. Just then the baby, which Tan had pushed to the back of his mind, stirred in the sling and began wailing. The woman shifted on her ankles, clucking anxiously, then produced one skinny breast that she popped into the baby's mouth. She moved the sling slightly to accommodate this action and Tan saw the baby's sharp eyes and square face, the thick shock of vertical hair that was not a family trait, the paler skin.

Tan looked to Bouman.

"Yes," said Bouman, "the father is Japanese, but she does not know who. She was not as lucky as me. She spent the war in Batavia as a comfort woman. She'd always wanted to go to Batavia, like her mother, for schooling."

"I am sorry," said Tan, stuttering over the phrase.

"Irony," said Bouman and smiled. "My greatest fear was that men would steal my girls, but look, ruined for anything, delivered permanently into my hands, given back to me, my lovely girls, by men."

Tan shook his head sympathetically. "She does not speak?"

"She," said Bouman, "has nothing to say."

The baby had fallen back asleep while nursing and Karen pulled up to the table, taking a seat and a bowl of soup close to Bouman's right elbow.

"Tell me," said Bouman, "what you plan to accomplish by this visit. I am no longer a trader, everything is gone, except for a small stash of gin and some rat poison."

"I will be honest with you," said Tan. "I thought you were dead. I was worried what would happen to Katrina, because of her Dutch blood. In Java, the Allies have herded all the Dutch into protection camps." Tan glanced sideways at Bouman, who, in the old tradition, was speedily slopping up his soup. "They have been forced to hire Japanese troops to protect them."

"Protect them?"

"From the Indonesians."

"Indonesians?" said Bouman, looking slyly up from the bowl. "And who are these Indonesians? Before we got here, there were no Indonesians. There were Dayak, Batak, Asmat—headhunters and cannibals selling their daughters for glass beads. And now, you are Indonesian? Can you tell me that you love the Balinese as brothers? That you find the negro of Irian Jaya anything but a terrifying barbarian?"

Tan felt a chill at the base of his spine. "What can I tell you that will satisfy you?" said Tan. "There is nothing just in this world, but some things are essential to improvement in the future and we must take the bitter to achieve the sweet."

"You speak like a politician."

"I am a politician," said Tan. "You would like something more direct? Your time has passed. You have profited in another's country, which is equivalent to theft, and I would rather see you leave, but could easily kill you and feel justified."

"You support the devil Sukarno."

"Sukarno," said Tan with a cryptic smile, "supports me."

There was silence after that, maybe a whole fifteen minutes without a word said. Karen stood up to spill more soup into everyone's bowl and Tan continued eating, despite the odd flavor, because he was tired of speaking to Bouman. Bouman was insane and this woman, Tan's daughter, and the little Japanese baby, Tan's grandson, were strangers and more than that, beyond the realm of his plan of noble return and rescue. What would he do with these people, inextricably bound to him by his own folly, by accidents of blood and union? Bouman was drinking a tall glass of gin. Tan saw that Karen too was drinking and thought of

THE CAPRICES · 118

his other daughters, perfect ladies protected in yards of fabric, manners. They would never recognize her and they would despise their father's indiscretion. Tan closed his eyes, unwilling to imagine further the sequence of ideas.

"Do you remember," said Bouman, interrupting the moment of peace, "how I once told you that if I had enough of this" — Bouman raised his glass — "that I would show you my fingers?"

"Yes, yes I do. I remember that."

Bouman got up and went to the far corner of the room, where the hammock was slung from the beams. Bouman ducked under it and began to rifle through some belongings that cluttered the top of a crude set of shelves. He lit a candle and long shadows began to dance across the wall, animated by each breeze that shivered the flame. Tan could see from the man's clumsiness that he had had a lot to drink. Karen watched her grandfather for a moment, her face softening, but then growing blank. She stood up and took the baby from the sling. She rocked it softly, then offered the baby to Tan. Tan was chilled. He did not want to hold the child; he shuddered, then realized he had never been in a position to be so cruel.

"I can see you love your baby," said Tan, finally relenting, extending his arms, and taking the child who, from his estimate, was about four months old. Karen smiled slightly, but her eyes were filling with tears. She snatched the baby back and began desperately cooing at it, even though the baby seemed peaceful and content.

Tan stood up. He had had enough for one evening. His blood pressure, he thought, must be soaring because he was dizzy and heavy pounding had begun in his ears. He was also a bit short of breath. He looked over at Karen. To his surprise, she too seemed to have difficulty breathing. Her lips were pulling at the corners and Tan saw that she had no teeth.

"Here they are," said Bouman with satisfaction. "Sit down, Tan. It will all be over soon."

Tan sat down. Bouman was holding a yellowed linen hand-kerchief. He unfolded this ceremoniously until the two shriveled, leathery fingers were revealed. The nails were brown with age and the fingers had curled, which made them look alive. Bouman set them down on the table.

"To what do I owe this honor?" asked Tan. He was feeling sweaty and weak. Something must have been off in the soup because his intestines were seizing up and he felt suddenly cold.

"This honor? I would like to be buried whole."

"Why?" asked Tan unsympathetically. "Are you dying?"

"We are all dying," answered Bouman. His voice sounded distant and muffled.

"Age," said Tan, "has made you philosophical."

Bouman laughed. "No, no. We are all dying. I have poisoned us by putting arsenic in the soup."

The next morning Aya crept into the compound. She had heard the Japanese were finally vanquished and was worried about the old Dutchman, who was an idiot and a drunk, but not evil. She also missed soap and cigarettes, which at this juncture she preferred to betel. Most compellingly, she wanted to know if Karen, who was a daughter to her, had survived the war. Many nights she had stayed awake with her heart pounding, vibrating down to her very wrists, remembering the soldiers dragging Karen by her hair as she struggled to get her feet beneath her. She remembered Bouman's strong arms holding her back, whispering, "Aya, they will kill her if we protest. Let them go. It will not be long before we are liberated."

Aya stood in the burnt square of what had been the house. Versteegh's dwelling was gone too. There was a cigarette half smoked, carelessly tossed into the ruins. She picked this up, smoothed it straight, then stuck it behind her ear for later. Bouman was still alive, still smoking, still wasting tobacco. There was a prahu anchored close by and on it she could just make out the outline of men moving about. Why would a boat be moored so close without Bouman in attention? Perhaps the Nationalists had taken over.

"Bouman!" she called. "Bouman, sir, where are you?"

In response, Aya heard the caterwauling of an infant. Aya's blood froze. The sound was coming from the manager's hut. She was not one to be overwhelmed by superstition, but her first thought was that a spirit was tricking her, using the most compelling sound known to woman to draw her into the hut. Who knows what evil awaited her there?

"Bouman, sir!" she called again. "Bouman!"

A canoe had set off from the prahu angling for shore. Aya watched the rise and dip of paddles, the sun glinting off black hair and sweating arms, the sun brightening the surface of the water in bladelike light and purple depressions. She felt the heat beginning slowly in the day, rising up through the earth. Aya found a match in her pocket that she had managed to secure before coming to the house. The baby was still crying. She lit the half cigarette. When it was burned clear to her fingers, she would make the short walk to the manager's hut. She would boldly greet whatever evil awaited her. She was an old woman and tough. Was there something stronger than she? What secrets and horrors were there that these old bones did not remember, recorded in the very stuff, ringed in the marrow and shell as years are told in the trunks of trees?

Colossus

THERE ON THE GUTTER the icicle hung down like an incisor. The afternoon sun shot through it, then flung the shattered light over the back wall of the porch. A steady drip muted by dead leaves on the step kept time with Jim's heart. And this tap-tap reminded him of something that he had once heard, but could not remember. The tide was low and despite the chill the odor of brackish rot was clear from the bay, while from the opposite side of the island, Jim could hear the waves exploding on the beach. At this near point, where Plum Island was two hundred feet wide, the honking of geese mingled with the low warning of foghorns. The dripping water punctuated the day's waning with its steady beat. On the mainland, the trees rose up like a purple wall, muted and unreal. Here, on this long sliver of barrier island, the land was squeezed tightly between a brilliant Atlantic sunrise and the bayside dip of a cool, evening sun.

The icicle was wasting into water.

What was that sound that he could not place? Was it the IV when Peggy spent that last week in the hospital, before they sent her home to die? He remembered the clear vein of fluid wasting itself into her arm, but the music of Peggy's illness was her harsh breathing and a beeping noise from some ineffective machine. No. Further back. Maybe when he was a boy. Maybe in his mother's kitchen. His mother's legs were traced over with veins and there were splinters in the kitchen floor. She was at the sink accompanied by a rush of water, something useful to complement her industry. He remembered his brother Paul's sniffling. Did Paul's life drip from him? Did his passing have a sound other than startling silence? No. Jim had seen life spill, pour silently into the earth. Blood left nothing but a stain—the heart left a knot of stilled muscle. Could the drip of the icicle be just that? A useless process of reduction? Jim thought of himself as having no more blood. He was as desiccated as the gulls killed on the causeway, which, within a week, were nothing but an oblong of leather with a few clinging feathers and a pair of blackened claws.

In the kitchen the radio halted between the football game and the storm, which had been brewing in the Great Lakes for days and was now heading east to Massachusetts. One town in Ohio had been annihilated by the storm's progression, but Jim had never heard of the town before and he couldn't remember the name. He understood the announcer's elevated voice and the force of the deafening wind, the sudden intrusion of static, but it was hard to feel the loss of something that Jim had never known was there. The air was consciously still and Jim watched a woman, parka pulled over her head, dragging an old black dog down the street. The dog's chain collar jangled as he bounced along. They disappeared where the elbow of the road curved left and soon Jim heard a door slam.

Some had evacuated the island. The rich routinely built houses on the beach, cathedrals on stilts reflecting the ocean in their glass faces, houses occasionally pawed off the sand by waves. But Jim's house was a genuine cottage, low and sturdy, sheltered by dunes. He had survived worse and there was no brick apartment in Boston for him to retreat to. He had no use for the desperate pleas voiced over the radio. Leave while you still can. Jim reinforced his windows with brown crosses of masking tape, neat and military. He secured the shed door with a web of rope. The wind would obey. The kitchen pantry was newly stocked with cans of beans, spring water, and a liter of Cutty Sark.

The Patriots were losing, 21–0, no relief in sight. Jim coughed to clear his throat, but the cough was unproductive and dusty. The storm massed itself to the south. The icicle stood sentinel, refracting with the precise brilliance of a rose window. Jim watched a gull beating slowly in the air. Just now, odd gusts like old spirits were coming on the street, tossing paper cups and old news, buoying leaves upward, then dropping the gull a good ten feet. The cold air was making Jim's hands stiff and there was a sharp pain in his lungs from inhaling it. Now it was time to go inside, but Jim felt himself pulled down. He sat down on a pile of greasy rags on the creaking wicker love seat. He was tired. He could not move. He was paralyzed.

The drip on the leaves continued and Jim thought he was drifting to sleep.

"Don't sleep," he warned himself. "You won't wake up."

There was a drip in his ears that echoed the sound of the melting icicle. Maybe his blood pressure was soaring. He should be watching that. Sometimes he heard his blood pushing on his ears. It sounded like even footsteps in the snow. Push. Push. There was a warmth extending from his feet up to his knees. He looked at his boots—duck boots from L. L. Bean. His feet seemed unattached. They could have been anyone's feet. His hand was resting on the arm of the love seat, which was fraying, trying to return to its original jumble of twigs. Jim regarded the spots on his hands, his fingers which were no longer straight, each headed in its own direction, his nails cracked and yellowed from a life spent in the stomachs of planes, under cars, prying apart riding mowers. Maybe that melting icicle echoed the drip of gasoline or oil from some tank that was no longer sound. Jim's nostril hairs were freezing. He watched the gull beat in place, first at ease, then with effort. Now it was being blown tail first, reeling in the face of the wind as if the earth were winding in reverse. The wind chimes beat against the house.

Was it possible that this dripping was him, something inside, wasting away? Some pipe that had rusted over the years? His faulty plumbing? Or maybe something from the war?

Jim had shipped out to the Philippines from San Francisco in November of 1941. He'd watched the other guys hugging their girlfriends after some wild nights — guys who had made the most of an opportunity where no girl would say no. He'd said his one goodbye, to his mother, weeks earlier, in New Hampshire. The leaves had turned red only in places. Everywhere Jim looked was lush and green. This last moment of summer seemed unreal, made him want to hold his breath. His hair was buzzed short and the sun felt good on his scalp. He was now Pfc. James T. Darcy of the 17th Pursuit Squadron, USAAF. The air force had a romantic pull.

"I don't like this flying around," his mother had said. "Stay on the ground where you belong." But Jim wasn't going to fly any planes, only fix them, and this had calmed her down.

The 17th Pursuit was stationed at Nichols Field, just south of Manila. Jim, like everyone else, had been stunned when the Japanese started bombing. No one did anything at first, just looked at the sky waiting for something more believable to come along. Jim watched a Japanese Zero cruise low, the bombs walk the length of the runway — BOOM, BOOM, BOOM — just like a giant stepping down the line. Pilots sprinted to their planes, only to see them burst into beautiful fireballs. Bombers taxied desperately, trying to get off the ground. The Japanese bombed with supreme precision. Their pursuits strafed across the wings of the American P-40s. No Japanese cartridge was wasted. An American pilot pounded his fists on the window of his cockpit, his figure slowly being erased by the smoke. There was too much to look at for Jim to make any conclusions; besides, he was in charge of a .50-caliber antiaircraft machine gun. Not that he was doing a very good job. Jim didn't know the lead time for shooting planes —the Zeros were speedy—so he sent shot after shot into the smoke of their tails, his bullets exploding as harmlessly as popcorn.

And then they had abandoned Manila. At the time, Jim felt an awful nostalgia for the place, even though he'd only been there a month. Even when the bombs had been blasting all around, in the brief spaces of reprieve Jim had heard music—guitar and happy Tagalog—just people singing and singing, crackly radio, clinking beer caps on the counter, women's hands clapping, and the kids yelling at the GIs to give them money, to meet their sister. And then the BOOM BOOM. On Christmas Day, the USAFFE forces had begun their retreat. There were not enough planes to justify an air force, so now Jim was in the infantry, in what was called Naval Battalion. The truck moved at an unsteady twenty miles an hour. The one road—Route 7—was clogged with the traffic of the retreating Americans. Jim had a rifle, an Enfield from 1922, and he cradled it in his hands. He was falling asleep. He was seated in the back of the truck with a bunch of other guys from the 17th Pursuit and a couple from the 14th Bombardment. Most of the guys were kind of quiet, passing around a bottle of lambonog, coconut moonshine, that a sympathetic local had felt the need to give them. Jim's head rested on the wall of the cab. He could hear the driver's buddy telling him a story.

"First guy dead in the Philippines, a nigger, no shit."

"What was he doing here?" said the driver.

"Passed himself off as white. I always made fun of him, called him 'Nig' because he was kind of yellow complected, always cracking up like a black boy. But I had no idea."

"What was his name?"

"Robert Brooks. I kid you not."

"And he was a Negro?"

"That's the honest truth." There was a pause, as if the buddy was taking a drink. "Hell, I don't care. That's one Jap bullet that didn't get me."

"That's what the war needs," said the driver.

"What?"

"More niggers. I wish one was driving this truck."

The Naval Battalion was in charge of protecting the beaches of Bataan from Japanese landing parties. Bataan was a peninsula that hung down from the mainland like a fat thumb. Sergeant Vinci set up a crude map and the men crowded around. He spoke loudly to be heard over the explosions, the constant waves of shrapnel that sounded like a bunch of quail going overhead. Sergeant Vinci had a creased, honest face. His delivery made him sound like a football coach, full of bravado and false encouragement. He drew arrows curving down from the mainland, showing the places where he thought the Jap boats would try to unload, places where the beach flattened out. Jim didn't think much of the strategy. If you saw a Jap, you shot him.

Jim thought Vinci must have kids because of the fatherly way Vinci treated him, but didn't want to ask him. Vinci really seemed to love his soldiers. It was an awful love. Vinci acted as if the fall of Manila was his fault, as if the hunger of his men was something he was directly responsible for. He would give the boys these emphatic claps on their shoulders, ask how Jim was doing, even though Vinci knew he was hungry and scared. Jim thought that Vinci wanted to touch all the guys to give them some kind of protection—the back slap that would render you bullet-proof.

But the men were dying all the same. When Bill Cruz of the 14th Bombardment took a bullet to the head, Jim found himself asking his brother, Paul, who had been dead for twelve years, to welcome his friend and show him the ropes. It was as close to praying as Jim had ever come. Off the tip of Bataan was the tiny island of Corregidor, a fortified rock connected to Bataan by tunnels. MacArthur and the other generals had been managing the death of their men, American and Filipino, from this point. And then they gave up. MacArthur left. Jim knew that they would not be evacuated now. The United States had written them off. They could all starve. They were battling away no longer for God and country, but for themselves, each man on his own trying to stay alive.

Jim pulled his eyes open. He saw again the bare sky and the empty bay. Across the water a lighthouse blinked—light then beam, light then beam—in time with the drip of water. He knew that sound. Was it the rain falling on the dense leaves of the jungle? A delicate drip into a pool, the ripples echoing in perfect circles? It had never been quiet enough to hear anything like that. Besides, he had not had time to listen. First he was fighting, then dying, then surrendering. They had lost the war, the Americans and Filipino Patriots, waiting for relief that never came. When had the battle ended? Jim had been sick and delirious when they surrendered. The paregoric was all gone. He had stayed out of the way of bullets, but the lack of food and foul water had conspired to finish him off.

Jim held those last days in Bataan and the Death March in flashes, like postcards of places he'd gone on vacation. He saw small events and vistas and had to write himself in because he knew he had been there. Jim remembered the sky and earth being one in the darkness. Then a fissure of red split the sky into two purple halves and the tops of the palms flashed green, a whistle and a crash, and then vacuous silence. This was surrender. The Japanese had won. He was now a POW. There was a Jap barking orders and Jim moved with the other men. They were moving north. Everyone was walking. Ten thousand Americans and sixty thousand Filipinos, walking. Those who weren't walking were dead. Jim stumbled along, keeping his eyes focused just ahead. There was a smell of shit. There was something dripping down his legs. The heat was intense, but this foul dripping was cold. He wondered if it had come out of him. He was only eighteen and thought that he was fresh, new. His mother had called his enlistment "a waste of sweet youth." She had been slicing apples for a pie and in his mind his sweet youth had become one with the smell of apples. He kept his mother's face before him as he walked. He remembered a Filipino throwing small green parcels into the path of the marching men. He could still see the GI next to him unwrapping the banana leaves and eating the rice. He could still see the Filipino man pleading for his life, the pistol shoved under his chin, his head exploding like a coconut hitting the pavement. Walking. Then the loss of a horizontal world. He must have fallen down. Vertical, everything was vertical, and he was surrounded by many pairs of boots. Then nothing.

He had been left for dead.

The moon shone a cold blue light and Jim could see a body lying in the road. A Filipino scout in bare feet but still uniformed. Jim could not see his face because the scout was lying on his side with his back to Jim. The scout was rocking back and forth. Jim wondered why a scout would do that, rock like a cradle, lie in the road. But wasn't Jim lying in the road?

"Hey," Jim called to the scout. "Where is everyone?"

The rocking stopped and from the far side of the scout's body, a startled dog raised its thin, black head. In its mouth was— string? No. Intestines. In the dog's mouth was the body of the scout, which was unraveling like a knit scarf. The branches rattled along the side of the road. Somewhere in the thick undergrowth were other black dogs with sharp heads perfect for digging around in the stomachs of fallen men. Jim was too weak to move. He watched the bushes. His heart beat against his ribs. Two figures emerged. Men. Two young men. Short and thin. Filipino. They came to Jim and squatted by him. One man reached into the pocket of Jim's pants. There was a startled gasp. He whispered something to his companion. Then, a cool hand that smelled of tobacco on Jim's shoulder. The face came close to his ear and whispered, "Boss, we take care of you now. Don't stop living, because I get mad if I have to carry more dead."

The Filipino men carried him to a house in a blanket for a stretcher, complaining all the way. Jim was over six feet tall.

"Man, you nothing but bones," said one of the Filipinos. The other one rattled some rapid Tagalog back, and the two men laughed. Jim was surprised by the laughing. "He says you all bones, but you have the biggest bones he ever see. And they're damn heavy."

The men carrying him were small. He was startled at their strength. He swung in the blanket and felt himself being rocked to sleep, like a baby.

Then he remembered.

Here was where he had heard that pervasive sound that echoed the drip of the icicle.

Jim had thought he was awake but he was asleep. Almost dead. And he heard nothing but that sound over and over. A drip that was not a real drip, but somehow muted. That sound was in his dreams playing softly from outside, while Jim—a child—watched his mother's marbled calves as she kneaded the bread. He sat on the floor. There was a draft and Jim coughed. His mother turned her great Flemish head to him. She was worried. Is this how Paul died? First a cough and then nothing? What was that rhythmic dripping sound?

And when he awoke it was April 1942. Jim was in the Philippines somewhere on the outskirts of San Fernando. A girl was standing across the room, a dark-skinned girl in a faded gingham shift. She was wearing straw slippers and had a weight of black hair that hung in a rope down her back. Jim was lying on a straw mat. The girl did not know that he was awake. She kept gazing out the window. She was eating dried watermelon seeds, cracking them in her teeth and spitting out the shells. When they hit the wooden bowl on the windowsill, they made a soft *plip* like water on paper. Jim had been listening to that sound in his sleep. He had never seen anyone eating watermelon seeds before. He didn't know what they were.

He asked, "What are you eating?"

She was surprised to see him awake. She stepped back, then smiled nervously. She looked around, for a family member Jim supposed, and then she said, *"Butong pakwan."*

Jim shrugged his shoulders. He didn't know any Tagalog.

The girl inhaled, nodded, trying to sort her words. She held out a handful of seeds to him. "Bones," she said.

Jim hesitated.

"Bones of the watermelon," she said.

He fell asleep.

When he came to, there was the girl, crunching watermelon bones, dropping her shells into the bowl. Jim was on the floor on a woven mat. The house had high ceilings. The sliding window panes were made of little squares of seashell. An old lady hustled in on bowed legs. She wiped her hands quickly on her dress and crouched over Jim. She sniffed him. The young man looked over at her and she nodded.

"Boss, she gonna make you something that taste like shit, but then you can eat. Make you better. Then I got some good news and I got some bad news."

But Jim was too tired for any news. In his sleep he heard the crunch of seeds and the girl's voice calling what sounded like "golly bear" over his head. Sometimes he cracked his eyes open. She poured the bitter tea into his mouth. In response to some yelling from the kitchen, she would say it again — "golly bear" and something else that he could not remember. He saw the girl poised over him. She had broad cheekbones and large, sad eyes. He would open his eyes and find her sitting there, keeping vigil.

"Sleep," she said. "Sleep now." And sometimes she picked up his hand that made hers seem like a child's in comparison.

In these hours of sleep, there was a time he was carried by the same two men who had rescued him in a blanket down the stairs of the house. They put him on a couch in the corner of the living room and covered him with thin cushions. The young man was talking to a group of children, girls and boys, skinny with big teeth. They were giggling and staring at him, but the adults seemed grave and frightened.

The young man put his head close to Jim's face. "Be quiet," he whispered. "Japs in town tonight. The children are going to sit on you. Be patient and please don't shit." And then it all went dark and Jim felt safe in the dusty air, beneath an old rug and some empty sacks. He felt the narrow rumps of the children weighted across his body and was happy, as if he might cry. Later he heard the old woman talking to the Japanese. He couldn't understand anything, but her tone was cavalier and she had a few Japanese words. The children wriggled along his spine.

The next morning, Jim was back upstairs. For the first time he found the young man's face familiar.

"Do I know you?"

The young man was smoking a thin cigarette. He nodded a couple of times. "Bataan," he said.

And then Jim remembered. He had accompanied Sergeant Vinci to the front lines. A thick rot wafted in with the evening breeze. While Sergeant Vinci was conferring with the officers, Jim had gone to find the source of the smell. Jim watched men passing him, to the right and close by, but no one seemed bothered like he was. He walked to the beach where the majority of the foxholes were. In the waves he could see dark clouds in the water, but as his eyes grew accustomed to the dying light, he saw that they were bodies. The arms moved with the waves, animated like a child face down in the shallows who circles with his hands so as not to scare the fish. The waves washed on the shore and the bodies bobbed. Jim backed away from the water. He could not be horrified. He did not have the time.

There was the scraping of a shovel in the dirt and with it the low muttering of Tagalog. He surprised the digging man by pushing through the bushes. A Filipino soldier was digging a grave. Beside the grave was the still body of a boy, maybe thirteen. The soldier leaned on his shovel. He was not crying but his eyes were full of grief. Another shovel leaned against the tree. Jim thought, Whose shovel is that? Was it the boy's? Was he supposed to assist in the digging of his grave? Then Jim thought that he should help. Jim began digging and soon the hole was deep.

"Your friend?" asked Jim.

"My brother," replied the soldier.

Jim thought he had been in the house with them for weeks, but it had only been two days. He felt better now. He said to his friend, whose name was Totoy, "I'm ready for the good news."

"You won't die. We stopped the diarrhea. We give you leaf from the guava tree."

"And now I am ready for the bad news."

Totoy shook his head. "I am sorry. You cannot stay here. They will find and kill you anyway here. And they will kill us."

Totoy's sister, whose name was Clara, was standing by the window. She was crying. She said something to Totoy, and brushed her face with the back of her hand, bothered by the tears. She was more angry than sad.

"What did she say?" said Jim.

Totoy took a deep breath. "She called me something. She says the Japs will kill you. She says we should keep you here."

Clara said something else.

Totoy sighed. "She says we might as well hit you over the head with a big rock. That would be better." Totoy shook his head. "Boss, you can't stay here. Look at her, look at my mother . . ."

"I understand."

"You are too sick to join the guerrillas."

"What will you do with me?"

Four days had passed since Totoy had rescued Jim and now it was time for Jim to leave. Totoy and two of his friends loaded Jim into a water buffalo cart and covered him with old clothes. It was the only cargo Totoy could think of that would not interest the Japanese. Old clothes were thought to be crawling with disease. The cart rolled behind where the Americans and Filipino soldiers had marched, and there were bodies everywhere. Jim thought maybe one would get up and live again, as he had lived after dying. Totoy's plan was to slip Jim into the camp, where he would at least be fed. It was only a matter of months before this war got cleared up, before MacArthur returned. Then they would have a big party. Totoy and Clara would come to pick Jim up, like parents going to get their kid at the end of summer camp. Jim went along with the plan and pretended everything was going to be all right. He had to believe it. He didn't have a choice.

To get to Camp O'Donnell took a day and a half. They caught up with some of the stragglers from The March a half mile from O'Donnell and waited behind a clump of stripped papaya trees. Soon afterward, a GI began screaming for water. He was dead then, although he didn't know it. His friends tried to calm him down, but the guards rushed at him and while the GI was beaten, Jim slipped into the crowd. He was half dead but standing, and in that was unremarkable. The water buffalo lapped its nose with its tongue and with a flick of its tail wished Jim good luck and goodbye. Totoy would not meet Jim's stare. He feels guilty, thought Jim, but he should not. Jim's pockets were full of guava leaves.

Jim thought of Clara in the camp, although they had not really talked. Her English was not bad, but she didn't like her accent, so she didn't use it. He had asked her, "What is *golly bear?*"

And she had conferred with her brother.

Totoy said, "It is American. Golly Bear. He is very big and is rescued by very small people. Like you. Very big. Like us. Very small. It is Clara's name for you. Golly Bear."

In his first few weeks at O'Donnell, Jim had daydreamed about the house near San Fernando. He wondered what it would have been like if he'd stayed there. He imagined himself growing strong, becoming a one-man army, a slaying machine who hid by day in the rafters, and by night picked off Jap after Jap. And Clara was a part of this dream, her soft hands and straight teeth. But after a couple of months, Jim only thought of food. The men were dying all around him. Beriberi. Malaria. Dark moods that made men sit down and never stand up again. He had seen a Japanese officer, the one they called the Frisco Nip because he had lived in California, decapitating Ned Thomas. Ned's body had been on the ground draining into the earth through his neck. Ned would not get up and walk, as Jim had, but Jim wished he would. He tried to raise Ned with the power of thought, thinking that if faith could move mountains, hatred must do more. But Ned didn't listen, just lay there. Jim imagined Ned's headless body going after the Japs, demanding the return of his head. He imagined all the dead men coming back from the burial fields, all those GIs and the million Filipinos, rattling on the gates of the camp, demanding compensation for their lives.

Jim's army of the dead coming to save him, take him away, had kept him alive. Now Jim found his dreams of salvation unsophisticated, even funny. He had been eighteen years old when Bataan fell. His idea of revenge was fed by comic books and movies. Jim had survived like a man, but had suffered like a child, bewildered and vulnerable. He had stopped counting the deaths of his friends when the number hit twenty. He had buried many more than that. He was lucky to be young, lucky that his brain could not fully comprehend the camp.

After O'Donnell, there was the ship to Japan. This was in late 1944, although Jim didn't know what year it was at the time. In the hold of the ship, ankle deep in water and excrement, Jim had made the journey to Japan. The light made its way into the hold only where rust had done its work. There was no place to lie down, no room to sit comfortably. The iron tub in the center of the room was used for water in the morning, as a urinal through the rest of the day. People died standing up, unable to rest even in death. Jim had no fear of boats in later years, but could not go to the movies. The darkness, the people packed so close, and the single shaft of light, took the breath out of him. Made him sweat and shake.

In Japan, Jim had worked in a steel mill in Honshu. The winter was cold and he had slept wrapped in a paper blanket. The men huddled together at night, sleeping like mice. The work details were long and many soldiers died with picks in their hands. The guards were armed with sticks. Jim thought there was something biblical about this labor. He remembered the Jews in Egypt, but thought he had it worse. The Jap supervisor was Sergeant Matsuo. Matsuo was tall and spoke in polite tones, but Jim never learned more than a few Japanese words. Matsuo oversaw the deaths of more than fifty men that Jim knew, but more somehow survived. And when word came that Japan had finally lost, these men rose up. Jim wondered what Matsuo's final thoughts had been when he was overcome by his crew of skeletons, half naked, toothless, and gray with dust from working so long inside the earth. They had pulled Matsuo from his quarters.

Jim had not been a part of the mob. He'd watched with others from a close distance, but all he could see was a tangle of emaciated limbs. Above the groaning labor of the men, Jim heard the creak of metal. When the prisoners stepped back, Jim saw Matsuo impaled on a six-foot drill that had been used in the mine. The drill stuck through his chest. Two men arranged Matsuo on his knees, so that his legs formed a tripod with the point of the drill, which was protruding through his back. In this way, Matsuo could stay upright. The soldiers placed him at the entrance of the mine, to keep watch, to guard that which he'd valued over all their lives. Sometimes Jim would dream of Matsuo propped on his drill watching over him, keeping sentinel on his life.

After the war, Jim got a job at a garage in Newburyport, just over the causeway from Plum Island. The first time he saw Peggy, he was pumping gas. She pulled up, with her boyfriend, in a brand-new, banana-yellow Buick convertible. Her boyfriend stepped out, needing to use the bathroom. He'd been drinking. Jim could smell that. The boyfriend had glossy black hair streaked with gray, but was probably only twenty-five. He had a slight limp. Peggy got out too. She stood a safe distance away and lit a cigarette.

"Your boyfriend's got a nice car," said Jim.

"The car's mine," said Peggy.

Jim wiped his hands on a rag. "Then why aren't you driving?"

Peggy laughed. She looked at Jim appraisingly. Jim started to get nervous.

"What time do you get off?" she asked.

The boyfriend had tipped Jim a whole dollar. He seemed like a decent guy. Jim spent the next hour trying to get his hands clean. When the convertible pulled up again, Peggy was driving. Jim hopped in. He took her for ice cream at the stand down the road. It was summer and gulls were wheeling overhead. Jim and Peggy were the oldest people seated at the counter. Kids in bare feet, their hair bleached with salt and sun, made up the other customers. Jim bought Peggy's cone for her.

He said, "I've got a dollar burning a hole in my pocket."

Peggy didn't talk much. Jim wasn't sure why he was there. He remembered that the girls in high school had liked him, but it didn't give him a whole lot of confidence.

"Was your boyfriend in the war?" he asked.

"Normandy," said Peggy.

"Is he a hero?" asked Jim.

Peggy was silent for a minute. She looked over at Jim, then away. "Twenty-four hours a day," she said. And that made Jim laugh.

Peggy was a hero because she married Jim, who had no money, whose only talent was fixing things. Her family set him up in his own garage. Peggy was educated, beautiful, and tough. She had smoked herself to death and never asked for pity. She'd married Jim because he was the biggest man she'd ever seen. She'd married Jim because of the reach of his hands and because of his huge feet with the gnarled toes that spread out like the roots of a tree. And he always let her drive.

This house on the island was Peggy's, had been in her family for a hundred years. She had supervised the replacement of shingles, barking out orders while Jim balanced at the top of a ladder. And Jim had built them a bed—longer by six inches than most—in the cramped bedroom, since Peggy didn't think it would fit through the door. Jim liked the island. He liked his garage, but the whole business of the camps was hard to forget. Jim had to consciously put all the deaths, the hunger, and the fear into the past each morning. This was a difficult task. Sometimes he felt he was living his whole life at once, in one moment, regardless of what was done with and what was left to do. Peggy didn't understand but was kind enough to act as if she did. She went to all Jim's reunions. She danced with his buddies, whose wives were dead, and then she died and no one danced anymore. They were in their eighties. They were all heroes because they didn't die and some were heroes because they did.

Peggy was dead six months when Clara had called Jim up. How Clara had found him, he was not sure. Must have been some veterans' organization. The connection was poor. Clara's voice sounded distant and blunted. Clara was unconcerned by the reach of years. She said, "I am so happy you are alive."

And Jim had said, "Me too."

Totoy was in San Francisco living in a hotel on Mission Street. He had come to the States for his veterans' benefits, which were not enough, and now Clara was worried. She was living in an apartment in Parañaque, on the outskirts of Manila, with her kids and grandkids. Totoy sent her money every now and then, but her cousin (who lived in Daly City and was Totoy's gambling partner) had written to her. Totoy's tuberculosis was getting worse. They were scared he was going to die and that, because he was in the States and didn't have enough money, they wouldn't be able to send his body back to the Philippines. He would be cremated.

"He will be like an old cigarette," said Clara. "What will God say to that?"

"I didn't know he was in the U.S." Jim had not seen Totoy since the day he'd been left at Camp O'Donnell. He'd thought of finding him after the war but hadn't known his last name or the exact location of the house where Totoy had taken him. Also, Jim had not wanted to find out that he was dead. "I'll go see him," Jim said.

Jim flew to San Francisco and stayed in the Best Western in Japantown. He arranged to meet Totoy at a restaurant in China-town. Jim was momentarily concerned as he looked down at the sea of black-haired men that he and Totoy would miss each other, but Jim, even though he was eighty, was still over six feet tall. His hair was a vigorous gray and stood a good inch and a half high on his head. Everyone was noticing him. Totoy would too.

Jim sat on the booth side of a small table with his great hands folded on the tabletop and waited. It was noisy and Jim was left alone with his thoughts, because no one was speaking English. He saw a pair of old men standing in the doorway and realized, as he did every now and then, that he was old like them. Then one man smiled. Totoy had cow eyes, like his sister Clara, and a broad shovel-shaped nose, and those were much the same as they'd been sixty years ago. Jim stood up. He recognized the work of years, but also what had been left behind. There was a nervous twinge in his stomach and he forced himself to nod and smile, as if he were at ease. Totoy was gray-faced. His hair was thin on his head and he'd made an effort to comb it over the bare spots. There was still black in with the gray. He was wearing a short-sleeved sport shirt that was tight across his stomach. The muscles on his forearms were pronounced but his upper arms were thin, like Popeye arms. Totoy was very weak and leaned heavily on his cousin, who was similarly dressed; the two men wore identical black, thin-soled loafers.

"My sister called you," said Totoy, smiling.

"Yes," said Jim, his hands forced into his pockets.

"This man," said Totoy to his cousin, "he buries my brother and now he buries me. But I, I brought him back from the dead."

And Jim remembered that Totoy was his dear friend.

Jim stepped around from the table. He didn't know if Filipino men hugged each other and he sure as hell knew that his guys didn't, but he wanted to hug Totoy. He wanted to bring him back from the dead and take him on a cruise, like he used to go on with Peggy, where you drank cocktails and watched kicking showgirls at night. He wanted to get Totoy a new shirt and a set of golf clubs, to bring him back to the island where they would sit on the porch and drink whisky. Because he was unsure of himself, he nodded a few times and sat down.

The menu was in Chinese but Totoy and his cousin had it figured out. They ordered neon-colored drinks with rice-flour balls floating in them. They ordered two kinds of noodles, one crispy, the other soft. They ordered little chicks that came served on an oval plate, lacquered a glossy red with the heads still on. Totoy mumbled to his cousin over the food in Tagalog, then looked over at Jim, his face large and happy. "I didn't think you would come to visit me. I think maybe you forget."

"No," said Jim quietly. "I didn't forget." There was an awkward silence.

"Tell me again," said the cousin, "how you two know each other."

Jim was sure the cousin knew all the details, but appreciated hearing it all again.

"On Bataan, Jim found me digging my brother's grave."

Jim was surprised at how plainly Totoy related the tale. There was no embellishment, yet it had already become a myth—the children sitting on the great couch, the cart ride, the water buffalo—as if at that moment all those things, and Jim and Totoy too, should have been flung into the heavens and recorded in the stars. Totoy's voice sang on and on, unwavering, over the staccato of the Chinese diners, over the slam of plates and the grinding traffic just outside.

"So Jim here wakes up," says Totoy, "and he wants to know, so he asks Clara, 'Who is Golly Bear?'" And the men broke down laughing. "Say it, Jim, because my accent is too thick."

"Gulliver."

"Golly Bear," says Totoy.

"Guliber," says his cousin.

Totoy nods in acknowledgment of his cousin's superior pronunciation. Then all the men laugh, which sets off the coughing, which brings out the handkerchief—white flecked with brown spots. And then there were new bright red spots. New blood. How could a man that old and sick cough such a vibrant liquid? How could his juices still be so sweet?

In the end Jim didn't invite Totoy back to the island. He gave him a check for a thousand dollars and told him to buy a plane ticket home. Totoy had no trouble taking the money.

He said, "I know I saved you for something."

Jim pulled the cousin aside. "Make sure he gets home. I told his sister I'd get him home."

"He either walks on the plane or he goes as baggage, but he goes in one piece," said the cousin.

Totoy shook Jim's hand firmly. "They are lying. I am still strong," he said, squeezing hard, the effort clear on his face.

One month passed and Jim heard nothing from Totoy or Clara or the cousin. He called the Philippines at 7 P.M. After three polite grandchildren in ascending age and fluency in English, he got Clara. There were roosters crowing in the background and she was barking out orders for breakfast. She didn't know who it was.

"Clara, it's Jim."

"Who?"

"Jim from the States. Remember? Gulliver?"

"Ah. Sorry. I am old and crazy." She yelled something and the house fell quiet. Even the roosters obeyed. "Totoy is dead," she said.

Totoy had died in San Francisco, destitute, surrounded by friends and relatives. Clara knew about the money for the plane ticket, but it had all been blown on gambling. For two straight weeks Totoy and his cousin had hopped on board the bus tour to the Indian reservation, drinking cognac, smoking Marlboros, and generally having a good time. Clara had a letter from the cousin. Jim was mentioned in it. The cousin had written Clara that Totoy didn't feel bad about the gambling. God wouldn't want him anyway and what Jim really owed him was a life. So for two weeks he had lived. Don't feel bad for Totoy. His last memory was rolling the dice and winning.

"So what do you think of that?" said Clara.

"I can't blame him," said Jim. "I wish I'd known. I probably could have come up with another grand to get the guy home."

"He is no good, that Totoy, even when he's dead. There were

pieces of bones in the ashes. In the airport, they saw the bones with the X-ray. They said the bones were seeds. Yes. Seeds to grow marijuana in dirt. I had to give the man at customs a thousand pesos."

The storm was picking up. A powdery snow blew in sideways. One by one the leaves had peeled away in the wind and now, at the base of the steps where the icicle had dripped, a flat patch of sky was frozen in the puddle. The temperature had dropped. The sun no longer broke through the veil of clouds. The once brilliant shards of light were now dulled with the promise of winter's occupation. The radio blared the news of a Patriot touchdown, but Jim had lost track of the game and didn't know if there was hope. A car hissed along the pavement and for one brief moment Jim saw himself reflected in the window, seated still as Lincoln and slowly turning white in the dying light. The wind shifted, blowing snow onto Jim's shoes and pants. The wind chime hanging by the door sounded a dolorous note.

Peggy had bought that wind chime in Rhodes ten years ago. He remembered entering the city in the late afternoon, siesta time. The heat beat down on the cobbled walks, glinting off the ramparts and washing every part of the medieval city in white light. All the wind chimes sounded together from the open storefronts and although Jim was ready to resist such calculated magic, Peggy had wanted a wind chime and bought one.

Peggy wanted to see Rhodes because she wanted to see all Seven Wonders of the World. The Colossus of Rhodes was one of these. The summer before, they had seen the Pyramids. But there was no colossus in Rhodes. When Peggy told him the statue was gone, had been gone since the third century B.C., Jim wanted to know why Peggy had made him leave Santorini. They'd traveled almost to Turkey on a ferry that reminded him of the death barge he'd taken to Japan in 1944, all to see where a statue had once been. Peggy found his reaction funny, but she found herself funny too.

"If you listened, you'd know the statue was gone," Peggy said. She stood at the port with the fierce Greek sun beating down on her. It didn't matter that the Colossus of Rhodes had fallen down in an earthquake in 226 B.C., been left in pieces for nine hundred years, then taken to Syria as scrap metal. She could still feel it. "There's something missing," she said. And that was enough for her.

The light was fading and the house across the street was now different shades of gray. Beyond the planks of the fence, the goldenrod was capped with snow. The beach plums and wild rose were lost somewhere in the snowy bank, and the tide had crept inward, floating a dinghy that now tugged at the rope. Jim could not move, only watch. Through the low hiss of snow skidding along the road, he heard a scraping noise as if someone were dragging a piece of metal—a lead pipe, maybe—up the street. He listened to the noise come closer. There was something frightening about it. Then, rounding the southern end of the street, he saw a man that he recognized. It was Matsuo, still impaled, carrying the drill up the street.

Jim watched Matsuo's progress as he drew nearer to the house. He remained calm. The drill tip scraped behind Matsuo, who struggled with each step. The drill seemed to throw his balance and the blunt end, still protruding from his chest, made the angle of his head unnatural, tilted to the left. A bloodstain bloomed general over Matsuo's tunic, like an awful flower. The drill was very heavy.

Matsuo raised his pale face to the porch and Jim noticed that Matsuo—unlike him—was still young. Jim held his breath and waited, but the apparition remained. The two men watched each other. After sixty years of searching, Matsuo had found him.

Finally, Matsuo pursed his lips and inhaled with great effort.

"*Senso,*" said Matsuo.

Senso meant war.

"*Owari,*" said Matsuo.

Owari meant finished.

Jim held Matsuo in his gaze, unable to look away. He asked, "Why are you here?"

Matsuo struggled to find words. He shook his head slowly. The wind sang through the scrubby pine. Still the radio sputtered on the kitchen table. The postgame coverage drifted out through the living room past the sideboard and the brown picture of Peggy's great-grandparents on the beach—their shaded heads and naked feet. There on the wall by the mirror were Jim's framed dog tags. By the door, on the loaded coat hooks, Peggy's barn jacket and slicker still hung. The wallpaper around the east window was peeling from the damp and needed attention. The gutter had filled up with leaves and sprouted icicles. To the north, the garage door of the neighboring house had blown loose and its even banging reminded Jim of his mother's skilled knifework as she chopped apples. Snow was collecting on the brim of Matsuo's hat.

"Why are you here?" Jim repeated.

Matsuo lowered his gaze. He looked up the road, then, clenching his teeth in pain, began walking away.

Yamashita's Gold

Twenty-eight years had passed since Carlos Salas had seen Pio Balmaceda. Salas was now a success: a citizen of Manila with his own rooms, a bank account, a respectable job of no distinction. The war had left him with the stiff-shouldered stoop of an older man well past his fifties, but in Salas this looked formidable rather than weak. He was popular with the bar girls—who found him quiet and easy to accommodate—since getting married was out of the question. For a man of his means, he was careful with his appearance. His linen suit bagged at the knees. His shoes were well shined, but the toes angled upward.

Salas stood leaning on the back of a bench, looking street end to street end for a taxi. He was unfamiliar with this part of Manila. His head was heavy and his expression subdued, indicative of a general weariness of life. His features were more Chinese than Malay, but in Quiapo—Chinatown—this was not unusual. In fact, the preponderance of Chinese and Chinese mestizos is why he second-guessed himself when he first saw Balmaceda (who was not Chinese, but was easily taken as such) across the street, through the smudgy window of a restaurant.

Balmaceda was eating a siopao. He raised the bun to his

mouth with small, ratlike hands. He nibbled at it, looking first to the right, then to the left. Salas leaned in closer (the street was not very wide), growing more convinced that it had to be Balmaceda. Salas abandoned his bench and crossed the street. He hid by a news vendor, shifting from one foot to the other to stop his back from seizing up, which it did when he stood for long periods of time.

This had to be Balmaceda tilting his head nervously from side to side as he ate, eyes ever alert to the possibility of a surprise, attack or otherwise. Salas remembered those awkward movements, remembered being bothered by them years earlier, when he and Balmaceda had spent long hours together. No doubt, Balmaceda's foot would be tap-tapping away on the linoleum, communicating his anxiety in code. Salas decided to slip away without confronting him. He hadn't seen Balmaceda in twenty-eight years, but it was more than this length of time that had kept them separate. Why would Salas approach him now? What would he say?

Halfway down the block Salas realized that he could have been wrong. What if it wasn't Balmaceda? The man he had watched was fat and had a slovenly bearing. What if it was someone else? Chinese were often mistaken for Japanese. Salas continued down the street, but he could not outdistance his desire to know for sure. He remembered Balmaceda looping little circles of despair with his twitching hands. He remembered Balmaceda's birdlike, sporadic gaze. The man's weight gain could account for the blunting of features. His stooped frame as he bent over his food could simply be the result of the march of years, or the absence of a military lifestyle that required a certain erectness. Faces and bodies changed, but people kept their mannerisms for life.

Salas paused beneath a flashing sign that outlined the shape of a bucking steer. Poor lettering in the window promised women and steak. He stood there thinking, until the impatient proprietor swung open the door, releasing chilled, smoky air into the street. He smiled at Salas; one tooth was outlined in gold and looked like an empty picture frame. Dance music boomed behind him. Salas shook his head.

Salas decided he needed a second look. By the time he got to the restaurant, the possible Balmaceda was gone. Salas took a chair at the table where the man had been seated; the view of the city was grim—a pharmacy, a few taxis, a tree beneath which street children gathered, all grayed and weighted by the sooty air. The traffic light turned red and children lit into the stopped traffic, tapping the windows with empty cups, their faces somber and dirty. Then the light turned green and they returned to their tree, flitting back like sparrows. Dead flies with their legs neatly folded littered the inside of the window. Salas drummed his fingers on the greasy Formica tabletop. Was it or was it not Balmaceda? A man in a dirty apron came out from the kitchen to take his order. Salas ordered a Coke, just to be polite, then asked the waiter about the man who had occupied his seat. Was he a regular? The man in the dirty apron thought this through.

"Are you sure you wouldn't like to eat?" he said.

"I'll take one siopao," said Salas.

"What kind?"

"Asado, I guess," said Salas, although he wasn't overly fond of it.

"Is that all?"

"Don't get greedy," Salas said. "It is, after all, a very small question."

"Monday through Friday for lunch," said the man. He returned a short while later with a small bottle of Coke and a steaming siopao.

"We have ice cream."

"What kind?"

"Queso."

Salas did not like cheese ice cream, but he figured this man had something to offer in addition to dessert. He stirred his ice cream, watching it pool into itself. The man in the apron looked closely into Salas's face.

"You were standing across the street."

"I was."

The proprietor nodded, satisfied. He handed Salas a folded newspaper. "This newspaper terrified him," he said.

Salas unfolded the newspaper. He gazed in disbelief at the front-page headline.

"He saw you watching him," said the proprietor. "He ran out of here the moment you left."

Salas returned to his apartment with the newspaper tucked neatly under his arm. He sat on his couch for close to half an hour with his right hand resting lightly on his brow before he finally unfolded the paper. The headline took up one half of the front page.

DISCOVERED BUDDHA ACTUALLY BRASS.

Brass. But this was impossible.

The newspapers had been running articles on the Buddha for weeks. An amateur treasure hunter, Rogelio Roxas, had unearthed the Buddha in Baguio, a city to the north, in a neglected tunnel of the Benguet mines. The cavern had been sealed with concrete, littered with human bones. This was the handiwork of the Japanese, who had looted every corner of Southeast Asia during the war. The gold had followed them to the Philippines. After the surrender in 1945, there had been many attempts to locate the hoard, the richness of which was impossible to calculate. The gold was said to be hidden beneath the streets of Manila, in the mountains of Baguio—even in the *Nachi*, a Japanese ship sunk in Manila Bay. This treasure had been labeled "Yamashita's Gold." Its existence was always disputed, shrouded in mystery—the stuff of legends and romantic idiocy. But Rogelio Roxas claimed to have found one of the caches. And he swore the Buddha was gold, hollow, and filled with jewels.

For a moment, Salas had no idea what to make of it. Brass? This confused him. Then he smiled, then he laughed. This was a puzzle, a deep, dark puzzle. The newspaper article went on to say that the statue was solid—which would make a jewel-filled cavity impossible. The statue was decidedly not Thai, but no possible origin was put forth. And this, yes, he understood. He understood Balmaceda's fear, his not wanting to see him. And who knew what trouble Balmaceda was in? The origin of the *brass* Buddha was somewhere in the Philippines, probably Manila. Somewhere in this sullen city an artist in a windowless room sculpted, sprewed, and vented. He probably was laid out on the floor now with a bullet in his head. There was still black wax beneath his fingernails. The hair on his arms was singed from the casting. Brass indeed. Of course, it was a phony. Not even a copy. DISCOVERED BUDDHA ACTUALLY BRASS carried the subheading "There Is No Yamashita's Gold Buried in the Philippines."

Salas continued reading. Despite his disbelief, he could not put the paper down. Rogelio Roxas was said to have dug the Buddha out of the ground while on holiday in Baguio. The newspaper did not explain why Roxas was digging in this particular location, nor did it attempt to consider the profound implications of finding a Buddha in country overrun with Igorot headhunters and dominated by Roman Catholicism. Salas was amused. After all, the real Buddha was pure gold and definitely of Siamese design. He knew this for a fact, for he had seen it. The statue was twenty-eight inches tall and weighed about two thousand pounds. The head screwed off, opening a cavity filled with precious stones—sapphires and rubies—mostly uncut and definitely Thai.

The last time Salas and Balmaceda were together, Balmaceda was crying like a baby, squatting in a puddle deep enough to reach his ankles. They had been in the cave for a week. Their rice was rotten and the roof was too low to allow them to stand. The

Japanese had been vanquished and now, robbed of the role of conqueror, Salas and Balmaceda found themselves living as primitives. There were bombs exploding all around, shaking dust into Salas's eyes. But that wasn't the worst. Salas couldn't even decide what the best-case scenario would be. He had never considered being taken prisoner. His mind would not even shape that thought. He knew why officers turned to their daggers, although he didn't believe the noble way out was necessarily noble. Sometimes killing oneself happened because of a lack of imagination. When an officer was stymied, he could always turn to Bushido, the warrior code, to guide him, and this code heartily endorsed *seppuku*. But what was the noble way for Salas? In his possession were the maps of the caves, the charts giving the location of the gold. He had orders to return the maps to the Japanese, so that when Japan eventually triumphed, they could retrieve their spoils. But lately, seeing his countrymen stacked like firewood, he had been having a hard time believing that the Japanese would necessarily triumph, even in the long years to come.

Living minute to minute was bad enough. Salas found Balmaceda repulsive. The two had not been friends in any real sense. They had passed time together, thrown into the same cramped circles by the necessities of war. Together, they had supervised the digging of subterranean vaults at Fort Santiago, an arduous task that had allowed Salas more than enough time to learn about his fellow officer. All Balmaceda read was military history: Alexander, Genghis, Attila—even Patton. He memorized battle strategies that he would never use; he held Hannibal's elephants in rigid admiration and hoped to one day do something similar, if there were elephants handy. His mind ran along its well-greased runners. His hair grew in an even, thick black carpeting. He bit his nails when he thought no one was looking, and blamed his copious tears on the poor quality of air in the cave. His intention was to survive the war with Salas, then await orders.

"What if they're all dead?" Salas asked.

"Who?"

"The men who would give you orders." Salas rather liked the idea of no one outranking him, but this depressed Balmaceda. "If we live, you and I, we will be rich men," Salas said, to cheer him up.

Balmaceda hadn't considered that.

They made their pact shortly afterward. Salas volunteered to hide all the maps—after all, such documents were very incriminating. He could be hanged just for having them. Balmaceda agreed. Sometime in the distant future, the two would join together. Some man somewhere would have an order for Balmaceda, and Salas and he would follow it. They would assemble a team of engineers and language scholars to decipher the maps' difficult coding. They would hire a team of workers to rival those of Cheops. Balmaceda would not move without Salas. Salas would not move without Balmaceda. Since until then the two men had been united in a similar cause, trust was irrelevant—betrayal unthinkable. Balmaceda drew his sword. He held it ceremoniously extended, which was awkward in their cramped quarters.

"What's that for?" asked Salas.

"A blood pact," he said.

Salas shook his head. "The war is over." The sword tip trembled. "I think enough blood's been shed."

Balmaceda let the sword drop and wept.

A month after they parted, Salas realized that one of the maps was missing. He assumed that Balmaceda must have it. Salas noted this fact calmly, even thought it to be an accident.

Now, he realized that map must have led Rogelio Roxas to the gold Buddha.

In the months that followed the Japanese surrender, Salas had too much on his mind to be concerned with the location of one map or of Balmaceda. Being Japanese was no longer an option. To stay alive, he had to forget the maps, the gold, even himself. He had to realize that he would never see his family again, and that if he were lucky enough to reach his next birthday, it was because he had been the beneficiary of an unfair and capricious god. He had to invent himself as the least of all mankind, one who would not stand out, who was unworthy of any attention—positive or negative—and once he had achieved this barefoot, straw-hatted anonymity, he could consider himself lucky. It was time to grow accustomed to the different stars, a laughing destiny that was mutable and had tumbled him off his victor's throne, stripped him of his garments, and delivered him—thick-tongued and thin-skinned—into the hands of barbarians.

Salas made his way to Manila as soon as he safely could. He thought living in a city would be safer and he was right. After the war, Manila was rebuilding itself, its people along with its streets. Losing oneself was easy. Not only that, but good help was hard to come by. Salas became a gardener, an expert on orchids and other flowering delights, and as he dug and potted, sprayed and tenderly wrapped the delicate blooms to the strong trunks of trees, he thought of the gold. All through the late forties and the fifties Salas longed to liberate the gold from its soft, loamy packing, to bring its brilliance back into the light of day. He thought of the tons of it, some in bars, the rest in jewels and works of art. Each brilliant bud recalled a more resplendent jewel, a tougher beauty, that was just waiting for its time to be liberated. The Cordillera Mountains, infested with headhunters, were also laced with the spoils of a brief and fallen empire. The cobbled streets of Intramuros delivered coded messages that would lead the informed hunter deep below the catacombs and caverns of the old city, whose wounds were slowly being stitched together with concrete and cinder block. Salas was obsessed with retrieval, but sometimes he wondered if this was more because of boredom than greed. The war had taught him about money and power.

Salas was for all intents and purposes a vassal, one of an army of houseboys, butlers, washerwomen, cooks, nannies, and maids. The garden sprawled out, intensely manicured in places, in others neglected with tangled vines on the wall and crumbling fountains overrun with toads. The main house had pillars like the White House and was a monument to fawning and bad taste. Salas only approached by the back door, which was unremarkable and less offensive to his aesthetic sensibility. He said little, which was blamed on his general lack of charm and his inability to speak good Tagalog; his employer and fellow employees assumed he had grown up speaking some Igorot dialect in Baguio. He shared a room with a ripe-smelling chauffeur and a houseboy. The houseboy had a guitar and the chauffeur had a drinking problem. This combination resulted in bad folk singing and loud renditions of movie pop songs. Sometimes there were girls outside the door to their room, sashaying back and forth on broad hips, their necks weighted down with cheap, heady blooms. Salas slept on a mat on the floor.

In the daylight, maids and washerwomen would slink back to work, their flowers dead, the bards of the evening revealed as the boors of the day. Salas worked with mister and pruning shears. His wards, the orchids, yawned lazily in his direction. He understood. Time passed slowly for him as well. Late at night, when his roommates had finally quieted, Salas would enter a deep meditative state. Below the earth's gentle crust, the jewels and gold bars waited, like patient bulbs in an eternal early spring. "Let them sleep," Salas whispered into the night, but what he really wished for was an end to his insomnia.

One particularly hot evening (the heat had sent him to his orchids for an evening misting) Salas noticed a bright light in the guardhouse. Salas stopped to watch. No doubt, something was wrong. No bulb or candle flame would beat so brilliantly against the walls. Suddenly the security guard darted out. He was burning, lit up, flaming, and his appearance was so stunning that Salas found it impossible to help him. The guard took three springing steps across the lawn. The flames whooped and snapped. He made it to the edge of the fountain, turned to Salas (who extended his mister to him), then disappeared, with a smoky hiss, into the lilies. It was as if the earth had swallowed him.

The following morning Salas found himself weighted by a dark mood. The other workers were all buzzing about the events of the previous night guard, of how Estanislaw, the security guard, had lit himself on fire.

"He was drunk," said the chauffeur. "He was reading comic books using a candle. The bottle spilled and then he must have knocked the candle over trying to get the rum."

"Is that all?" asked Salas.

"No," said the chauffeur. "When they went into the guardhouse, they discovered the boss's missing watch. The security guard has been stealing things."

"That doesn't surprise me," said Salas.

"They're going to search our things, the maid heard the boss's wife saying . . ."

"When?"

"After lunch."

Salas packed his things. There was nothing to directly incriminate him. There was the good-luck scarf written over with Japanese characters, a gift from a well-meaning village, but he could easily argue that this had been lifted off a dead Japanese officer. He could conceal the information to the security box, where he had placed the maps for safekeeping, but the idea of having his belongings rifled through bothered him deeply. Any scrutiny did. Besides, he was now old. He had already wasted much of his life as a servant. This was a sign to move on. He passed Estanislaw—who was bandaged like a mummy, glumly being questioned by the boss's eldest son—and caught a jeepney downtown.

Salas found work at a multinational corporation that made

shampoo, soap, and toothpaste. He spoke Japanese and was, therefore, useful.

Salas awoke early on Saturday morning, the day after he had seen Balmaceda. Salas sent his servant, Fernando, a handsome boy with feet like a duck, to buy the paper and some pan de sal. Other than Salas's eagerness for the paper, this was all routine. As Fernando descended the steps, he no doubt thought that Salas had started on his careful straight-edged shaving. After that, Salas would choose a short-sleeved shirt, find weekend socks to match, finish off with light trousers, then head in slippers for his small balcony to tend his small orchid garden. Fernando did not expect to be accosted on the steps when he returned. Standing in the dim light of the stairwell was a tall, dark-skinned man who, despite the heat and the shadowed light, was wearing sunglasses and a long-sleeved jacket and tie, American style.

"You work for Mr. Salas?" asked the man.

"Who wants to know?" asked Fernando.

"Just give him this. He will understand."

Fernando accepted the envelope.

Salas had heard voices on the stairs. He was nervous and when he poked his head out of the doorway, he caught Fernando shaking the envelope, checking the seal.

"Who gave you that?" asked Salas. Fernando looked down the stairs in response. When Salas peered over the edge of the railing, the stairwell was empty. He heard the door clicking shut as someone left the building.

Salas ate his roll. The envelope was on the table; he regarded it as he chewed. He did not open it, nor did he unfold the paper. Fernando peeked around from the kitchen. Today Salas would send Fernando to the movies with five pesos in his pocket, for supposedly good behavior. And after that, Salas would tear open the envelope and find sixty thousand pesos in new bills.

There was no explanation for the gift. Salas could only guess. Clearly Balmaceda had recognized him and maybe Salas had been followed home. Who knew what group Balmaceda was running with? Probably someone wealthy and powerful. This gift said a number of things. It said, "We know who you are and that you have the other maps." It said, "We have the resources to excavate the gold." It said, "We will make you rich if you cooperate."

Who were these benefactors? According to the papers of the previous week, Rogelio Roxas's gold Buddha had been confiscated by members of the president's family. The president. That would make sense. Salas thumbed the stack of money and its exquisite flutter made him giddy.

Salas headed straight for the tailor up the street who offered same-day service. It was still early. Who could blame him for wanting some new clothes? He ordered a suit, buff-colored linen, double breasted and fully lined, which was ready at six that evening. Salas dressed at the tailor's and took his old clothes folded in a brown paper package tied with twine.

Salas's shoes were brand-new but he decided to have them polished, just for the pleasure of it. The shoestand rose regally off the street, with metal platforms on which to set one's shoes. He took the leftmost of the three seats, which were worked by three kneeling boys. Salas drummed his fingertips on the worn wood of the chair's arm; this lightness was strange to him. He owed his joy to some whim of fate, which left him feeling both lucky and nervous. Beside him, a man ruffled the pages of a newspaper, reminding Salas he'd ignored the paper this morning, its offerings overshadowed by more immediate good news. The man snapped the paper down and looked at the boy who was coating his shoes with polish.

"Cordovan is not brown, you idiot," he said. The boy quickly raised the polish tin, which clearly stated *Cordovan* on its lid. The boy returned to his work. Salas looked away before the man could see he had witnessed the mistake. The man harrumphed over his mustache (he was part Spanish, no doubt, to grow facial hair like that) and trained his eyes on Salas. "What do you make of it?"

Salas raised his eyebrows. Surely he could not be referring to the shoe polish.

"The Buddha, the gold Buddha," he said.

Salas shrugged. "Is there something new about it in the paper?" he inquired casually.

"Fascinating," the man said, "If you find such stuff fascinating, treasure hunting, gold and the like. Anyway this Mr. Roxas insists that the Buddha he dug up in Baguio is gold. Doesn't know where this brass statue came from at all. Roxas claims that the president's thugs stole the gold Buddha out of his house. That, of course, is not in the paper. I heard it, well, somewhere." Here, the man stopped to consider his audience.

Salas was delighted that the man, obviously wealthy, was speaking with him. He attributed this to his new shoes and suit. "I feel certain the Buddha was gold," Salas said. "You know, I'm sure, all about General Yamashita's retreat."

"Yes. Backwards out of Manila, and MacArthur advancing all the time. Yamashita finally stopped up around Baguio. He was executed, wasn't he?"

Salas nodded. "Hanged. For war crimes." And then he smiled. This was uncontrollable.

"There's no doubt that he buried some gold up there," continued his companion, "but how much? And why hasn't it all been retrieved?"

"One hears rumors . . ." Salas checked his audience. The man was deeply interested. "They say that all the locations are booby-trapped. Bombs will detonate if the precise directions for retrieval are not followed."

"Well then, how do you get the gold?"

"There are maps—specific engineering instructions for the retrieval. These maps are still in the possession of the Japanese."

"You don't say."

Salas nodded. "The maps are in an ancient Japanese dialect that has not been spoken for over a thousand years."

"You don't say." The man smoothed his mustache. "Who did the work?"

"Work?"

"The digging."

"Oh." Salas grimaced, but quickly corrected his features. "POWs, I should think."

"Wouldn't they have spoken out?"

"Well yes, if they were alive. I've heard . . ."

"Yes?"

"Well, nothing at all on that matter. Maybe they're all dead."

"All of them?"

"Yes." Suddenly Salas felt weary. "But these are just rumors, of course. We know the Japanese looted all the way from Manchuria to Manila. No one will admit to having the money. Stories are created."

"The money's probably all back in Tokyo."

"Or Switzerland. Who's to say there's any Yamashita's Gold at all?"

"But if there was . . . , ho ho ho," said the man. He flipped the paper so that Salas could see the front page. There was a picture of an innocuous, bespectacled man.

"Who is that?" Salas asked.

"That is Roxas. He's speaking at Plaza Miranda on Saturday, at the Liberal Proclamation Rally, along with everyone else who has a problem with the president."

"He should keep quiet," Salas said.

"You're right. He won't live long with an attitude like that, not under this administration. What good is gold when you're dead?"

Salas took a taxi, smiling to himself as he passed the crowded jeepney stop. What he needed was a new nightclub to match his new affluence, not this dive that he had been frequenting for the past ten years. No doubt, when he actually brought forth the maps, he would be a rich man. Sixty thousand pesos was fine as a gesture of goodwill, but a small amount nonetheless. He would worry about lifestyle changes later. The old nightclub had a measure of comfort that he appreciated in his own way, and besides, who better to appreciate the new wealth than someone who had seen the old poverty? He would ask for Lina, who was near forty and practically in retirement, but she had known him longest and she would be the most impressed. In fact, it was his desire to impress Lina that caused him to abandon the taxi and proceed on foot up the alley that led to the rear entrance to the club. He would tap on Lina's window. She would be confused at first, but then she would see—new suit, new shoes . . .

Sneaking up on anyone is something that one should carefully consider. Sneaking up on a prostitute, even one near forty who is practically in retirement, is never a good idea, but Salas felt light and was therefore lightheaded. He walked up the side of the alley, with the tapping step of new soles. The shoulders of his suit were padded to make him look broad and strong, less stooped. How effective this actually was is not of importance, because Salas believed in his shoulders just as he believed in the faithfulness of the long-buried treasure. The gold was his, after all, had been his for twenty-eight years.

At first, Salas didn't hear the other's footfalls. The alley was deserted. His sobering thought was that his newfound prosperity had impressed someone else, someone who had followed him into the alley, which usually had a few inhabitants—tired women wringing out nylon hose, or their unwanted children busy in a coin-tossing game. Salas stopped behind a parked car, and as he'd predicted, the steps too stopped. In the reflection offered by the rear window of the car, he saw the outline of a man—tall and thin, and that was all because the light was poor and the window dirty. Slowly, he turned around.

Salas did not recognize the man because he did not want to. He registered that the man was unarmed and that he did not have a threatening demeanor. He wore loose trousers that had holes in the knees and were shredded at the cuffs. His shirt was filthy and the sleeves had been pulled from it. His eyes were quiet and questioning. He wore no shoes. At first Salas refused to recognize the man, but then he found his presence undeniable. This man was Dr. Santos, a civilian imprisoned in Fort Santiago whom Salas had known during the war.

Salas began to sweat, even though he felt suddenly cold. He forgot his errand, where he was. His mind folded in upon itself, and next thing he knew, he was stumbling into the chill of an expensive restaurant, having left the alley and run across a busy street. He was not damaged physically, although he had been narrowly missed by a number of cars and jeepneys. The waiter touched Salas's elbow in a warm, yet polite way. He guided Salas to a chair.

"What has happened, sir?" asked the waiter.

Salas shook, unable to answer.

"Are you hurt?" The waiter gazed into Salas's face. "Were you attacked?"

Salas nodded, although he knew this to be a lie. This was the closest he could come to describing the feeling he had, the terror that he had taken with him from the alley and into the restaurant.

"Shall I call the police?" The waiter knelt at Salas's side and fanned him with a menu. Salas shook his head. How could he tell this man—or anyone—that he had seen a certain Dr. Santos, a man he had once met and seen one time afterward, whom he knew nothing of except that he was a skilled surgeon and that he was dead.

The waiter placed a drink in Salas's shaking hands. He sipped it—a good scotch—and thanked the waiter for his solicitude.

"A gift, sir," the waiter replied, "from Señor Ocampo. He would like for you to join him."

Salas looked across the room. Señor Ocampo was the Spanish mestizo with whom he had chatted while having his shoes shined. The rest of the scotch was in a bottle on the table.

"I hear you were mugged," said Ocampo. "It's terrible, it is, but you know, this city, this country, has always been like this. It hasn't gotten worse. A cesspool."

"Then what they say about you mestizos is right," replied Salas.

"And what is that?"

"Enough distance to see the problems in the Philippines and too much love for the country to ever leave."

Ocampo laughed heartily. "My father was pure Spanish blood, third generation. His mother cried for a month when he said he was marrying a Filipina." More hearty laughter followed. Ocampo poured Salas a generous glass. "I'm buying you dinner," he said. "The thing to order here is *lengua*."

Salas did not want to be alone and this Señor Ocampo was certainly good company. A few glasses of scotch had soothed Salas's fear, although he still felt a nagging generalized wariness. Ocampo was in the sugar business. His wife and children lived on the island of Negros, in Bacolod, and while on business in Manila, Ocampo considered himself a bachelor.

"So what's your story, Salas," he said. "Who are your people?"

Salas laced his fingers together. He knew his history well.

"Mine is not a happy story," he started. "I was born in Baguio in 1915. My father was a carpenter."

"Same profession as Our Lord's."

Salas smiled. "Yes. There were eight of us children at one point. We had little money. There were only four of us still living at the start of the war."

"How sad."

"The Japanese finished us off."

"Except for you, of course."

Salas almost laughed. This was not the first time he'd forgotten to include himself among the number. "My mother died in
childbirth. There was"—here Salas looked thoughtfully at his
entwined hands—"a good deal of blood." He looked up at
Ocampo. "I found her. The baby miraculously survived. He was
covered in hair. The local mystic said this was a good omen."

"Ah, but the mystic was wrong," said Ocampo with deep-felt
sympathy.

"Wrong?"

"Well, yes. The child died in the war."

"That's right," said Salas. "I mean, right in God's eyes. We
must accept his decisions."

"You are a man of faith!" declared Ocampo.

"Well, I was raised by nuns—a Belgian order in Baguio. They
taught me English, introduced me to books. She was a good
woman."

"She?"

"Sister, Sister Mary. She was a good nun although she had a
drinking problem and . . . and a mustache. She also had a
wimple." Salas traced the wimple with his fingers extending out
from his head.

In response, Ocampo stroked his mustache. "And where is she
now?"

"The Japanese . . . Unspeakable, you know. Even though she
was a nun . . ."

"And even though she had a mustache!" added Ocampo. Here
they fell into awkward laughter, much controlled, yet impossible
to completely suppress. "I'm sorry. I'm an insensitive drunken
boor!" said Ocampo.

"No, no," said Salas, patting the man on his arm. "She would
have wanted it this way."

"Ah." Ocampo filled the glasses and raised his to clink with Salas's. "To Sister Mary."

The following morning, Salas was awakened by the ringing of the phone, but he did not answer. He was exhausted from the previous night. He had been tortured by bad dreams, nightmares brought on by scotch, and some mild form of hysteria activated by a change in life, or so Salas argued. A prisoner had come at him in his very bed, this bed, with the rumpled sheets. This skin-and-bones apparition had no head. He also had no shirt, and his bare chest revealed each rib in clear detail, a delicate vault of bones that arched above his flat belly. The navel was stretched open—then blinked: an eye in this unlikely location. He held a sword high above his shoulders. His belly-eye was trained on Salas. Salas counted his final seconds, and then he was back in Fort Santiago in the caves with Balmaceda. All kinds of prisoners were digging, Filipinos and Americans mostly. Balmaceda was making his way through the deep tunnel with a little silver mallet. The prisoners shifted soil to the scrape and scrape of shovels.

Balmaceda, on impulse, took the mallet and cracked it across a man's skull. Instantly the man collapsed. None of the other prisoners seemed to notice. Salas went over. The man's skull had split cleanly in two. Balmaceda separated the halves, like two hemispheres of a cracked almond. Balmaceda plunged his hand deep into the brain meat. When his hand came out, bloodied and trailing stringy gore, he held a stone. It was a ruby, uncut and blood red. Then Salas realized that the scar on his stomach had started dripping blood, then trickling. He covered the wound with his hands.

Salas dressed quickly. He had slept until noon. He looked at the table. The pan de sal and coffee were cold. Fernando was sulking by the kitchen door with a black eye.

"Why didn't you answer the phone?"

"I just missed it. I'm sorry, sir," said Fernando, whose sweat was still thick with coconut liquor.

Salas took a jeepney to Quiapo. He had the jeepney let him off around the corner from the restaurant where he had seen Balmaceda. He straightened his shirt and combed his hair in the reflection of a parlor window. On the front page of the paper was something about the Liberal Proclamation Rally at Plaza Miranda the following week, but this was dwarfed by a headline describing a restoration project in Intramuros that the first lady had decided to oversee. The engineering firm that had won the contract bid was Japanese.

"Sir, fifty centavos," said the paper boy.

Salas gave him a five-peso bill.

The restaurant was busy on Sunday. Salas took the same seat by the window, wondering if Balmaceda would turn up, even though he usually only came during the week. No matter. Salas felt a solidarity sharing this seat. Hundreds of sparrows shot through the air. Salas had always hated the sparrows. They symbolized Manila to him—Manila, whose calcified lungs coughed up the little birds much as a consumptive coughed up blood. A waiter came to take his order.

"Where is the owner?" asked Salas.

"On Sunday, he is with his family," said the waiter.

"Do you work here during the week?"

The waiter shook his head. He was a student at Santo Thomas. He had a scholarship. Salas participated wearily in this accidental conversation, wolfed down his siopao, nodded hastily as he got up from the table, pressing a tip into the student's hand. He headed for the door, having momentarily forgotten the purpose of his visit.

Then, across the street, Salas saw Dr. Santos again. He was leaning with both hands on the back of the bench in exactly the same attitude Salas had on the day he sighted Balmaceda. Salas jumped into the street, this time confused into pursuit. A jeepney screeched to a stop, then was quickly bumped another half foot by a bus that had been following close behind. Salas was knocked down, although uninjured. He saw the back of the doctor's head disappearing down the street, just slightly above that of the average-height man, but as he was now lying on the sidewalk, there was nothing he could do.

When Salas returned to his apartment, a soldier was standing in the hallway and his door was open. He paused at the top of the stairs. Fernando, who was at the end of the corridor watching, shrugged apologetically.

"What are you doing?" Salas inquired of the soldier.

The soldier raised his eyebrows, then hissed through the doorway to alert the others to Salas's presence. A man in a nylon sport shirt and white slacks walked casually into the hallway. He was wearing dark, square sunglasses. His shirt was tight across his belly. His skin was dark, nut brown and shiny, even though he was not sweating. He smiled broadly.

"Do you like the apartment?" Salas asked.

"Who are you?" the man replied. He was holding a handful of mail that Salas had left on his desk unopened. It was open now. The man sorted through the envelopes. "Salas? Is that your name?"

"Carlos Salas."

"And you are from . . ."

"Baguio."

"Baguio?" Here the man laughed. "I do not think you are from Baguio."

"I know what you're looking for." Salas walked past him and into the apartment, which had been thoroughly searched. Every drawer was overturned. The crash of papers reached him from the other room. A soldier who could not have been more than sixteen years old was slashing the underside of an upholstered chair. "They are not here."

"Where are they?"

"I will give them to you, but not now, not here."

"Where then? When?"

"Somewhere public."

"Plaza Miranda," the man said. "Saturday night. Nine-thirty."

"The Liberal Proclamation Rally?" asked Salas.

"Why not?" said the man. "I have business there anyway."

The man did not whistle to his men and leave. He set a chair upright and sat, then offered Salas a spot on the couch—the cushions were all slashed—across from him.

"How did you get the maps?" he asked.

Salas studied the man. He wondered how much he knew and which version of his past would be believed. "When the Japanese occupied Baguio, it was natural that they would need house help. I spoke a little Japanese—my father, a carpenter, was Japanese, although I was brought up Filipino. Catholic, of course." The man responded to this with a smile. "I was in charge of keeping General Yamashita's office. When Baguio was being liberated, there was chaos—many distractions. I stole the maps."

"Alone?"

"No. Another servant helped me. His name is Pio Balmaceda." Salas glanced up at the man. "I think you know him?"

"Yes. He is staying with us." The man seemed satisfied. "I am sorry if we have inconvenienced you," he said. When he reached the doorway, he turned to smile at Salas. "Your friend, Balmaceda, has already confessed to being Yoshimi Akihiro, a private in the Japanese army."

But Salas had the last laugh. This man did not know everything. Balmaceda, or rather Yoshimi, was not in the Japanese army, but the navy. Yoshimi was not a private, but a commander, second in rank to a rear admiral. Salas knew because this was his rank. They had served together, side by side, with many men at their disposal.

• • •

On Salas's twenty-eighth birthday, August 30, 1942, his appendix burst. He was in Manila at the time recovering from duty performed in the Solomon Islands. He had been in pain for a number of days. He thought he was suffering from an acute case of indigestion brought on by eating too much native food, which favored garlic and chili. When the appendix burst, the pain was intense to the degree that Salas could not scream—only moan. He moaned loudly for close to an hour before he finally managed to alert someone to his bedside. The Filipino servant was very distressed to see a superior bathed in sweat, shaking uncontrollably. He resisted the desire to run, finally crouching beside the bed so that Salas could whisper his condition into his ear, as best he could describe it.

"I am dying," he said.

Perhaps it was the servant's fear that he might somehow be held accountable for Salas's death that made him suggest the Filipino surgeon, who was a prisoner at Fort Santiago. Of course, Salas (whose real name was Kamichi Ayao) would have preferred a Japanese doctor, but in retrospect the fact that none were immediately available probably saved his life: he did not need a leg sawed off nor a bullet tweezed from his buttocks. Salas remembered opening his eyes to see the doctor at his side. The doctor was thin from imprisonment. He had large, kind eyes. He palpated Salas's stomach as gently as possible with hands that did not shake. Then he gave Salas a shot, and as he slowly faded from view whispered in his ear, "It is only the appendix. I have done this at least a hundred times."

This reassurance is what was rooted in Salas's mind. The doctor, Dr. Santos, was a prisoner. He had to do what was asked of him, without questioning. His life depended on Salas's survival, but his words were said in kindness. Later, when Salas was recovering from the surgery, he found a scrap of paper concealed in the pocket of his shirt. The shirt had been laundered, but somehow the message—although badly faded—remained legible. It said, "My son is Arturo Santos in Fort Santiago."

The doctor must have put it there.

How many messages were enclosed in this one? It is hard to say. Definitely "Please save my child," or "You can return my favor," or "I have hope when there was none." At the time, feeling munificent, Salas actually had someone look Arturo Santos up. Yes, he was at Fort Santiago. He was eleven years old. And that's all. What else could one learn about an eleven-year-old boy? That he was short? That he was thrilled by cars? That he used his sleeve in place of a handkerchief?

Salas was sure that he could have done something to ensure Arturo Santos's survival, but war makes one negligent of lives, particularly those that are not useful in any way. The scar healed. Salas could tell women he'd received it in battle. Why not? He had earned it at the hands of the enemy.

Salas forgot about the doctor. He forgot about his son. Years passed. The battle was no longer offensive, and now the unthinkable—surrender—was being planned in detail. Yoshimi and he were in charge of supervising the burial of a cache of gold bullion, reportedly the spoils of Yamashita's march down the Malay Peninsula. Salas remembered Yoshimi's boots that morning. For the first time ever, there were smudges on the toes.

Digging had started on the caverns months earlier. Only a handful of officers knew what they were for. MacArthur was already in Manila. Perhaps MacArthur had expected the Japanese to throw up their hands in exasperation and start packing. Their presence in his old neighborhood infuriated him, but Salas and the other men were under orders. MacArthur began shelling Manila; the corpses—nearly all Filipinos—filled the streets. Dogs, who had not been seen to roam the city in months, suddenly appeared well fed.

Yoshimi (now Balmaceda) was coordinating with the engineer and—strangely enough—the language scholar, who had been instructed to translate the maps into an obscure Japanese dialect that had not been spoken for over a thousand years. The scholar was a tall, thin man with large watery eyes. His hands were large as well, and hung loosely on his wrists, as if they were a marionette's. Salas couldn't remember what the dialect was called, too obscure even for an educated man to be familiar with, but it was the bane of Yoshimi's existence. There was no word for "mine," "bomb," or even "wire." The treasure was to be booby-trapped by a complicated series of incendiary devices and explosives. The happy treasure hunter armed with nothing but a shovel would not get far; with a bulldozer he'd be blown sky high along with the surrounding city block. One needed the maps to have any success at all. In the end, the scholar translated that which was translatable—sometimes resorting to homonyms, sometimes approximating meanings. For example, since there was no word for "prisoner," he substituted the word "slave."

Salas was in charge of organizing the POWs into functioning work crews. Most of the men were sick, and in other circumstances probably would have been impossible to move. But the sound of shells exploding all over Manila gave these walking cadavers hope. "Dugout Doug" had actually returned, as promised, and they were not going to compromise their chances at freedom at such a close juncture. Americans, Australians, and Filipinos lined up side by side. The hollow look was gone. They shouldered their shovels in the war's twilight, much as they'd borne arms at its start. Salas could feel the stifled excitement, the hope. He remembered an Australian soldier whose eyes actually twinkled in his gaunt face. His shirt had rotted to a comic effect: all that was left were the sleeves and the collar, held by a narrow strip of reinforced fabric that laced them together across his shoulders. As he passed Salas, entering the mouth of the hole, Salas heard his thought, "Last thing I'll do for a Jap." And it was.

The first day's digging went without a hitch. All the prisoners were shot at the end of the day, as Salas had previously decided.

The following day, one of the bombs went off, killing a Japanese officer. The engineer was furious, but didn't explain his anger to anyone. He left to make another bomb, and the Japanese officers waited and waited. Three days they waited in Fort Santiago. The smell of rotting corpses lay over the entire city in a thick smog. Everyone was sick. MacArthur's bombs exploded with the *thud thud thud* of a beating heart. Salas got used to it. Finally, the engineer corrected the problem and presented Yoshimi with a lovely bomb, but when Salas sent the POWs back down into the ground, the gas from the rotting corpses of the men he'd killed the first day made them ill, and they could not dig. Yoshimi pulled him aside. This was Salas's responsibility. The prisoners were sitting in rows at the mouth of the hole. They looked at Salas with pouchy, alien eyes as if they too were admonishing him for failing to complete the work. At the end of one of the rows, carefully wrapping another man's foot in a rag, was Dr. Santos.

Perhaps it was the fact that Salas hadn't slept in over seventy-two hours, but the thought of facing that man bothered him deeply. He would rather have faced MacArthur. Salas was feeling unfamiliar pangs of guilt. He knew the war was lost, and now, no longer secure in the role of victorious naval commander, he had been considering his worth as a man. Salas watched unnoticed as the doctor wrapped the wound, which was badly infected—swollen a dark purple and wet with pus. The injured man, another Filipino, waved flies from his eyes in a passive way. He shook his head, which the doctor did not see. Salas took this to mean that he knew that tending his injury was hopeless, but still appreciated the doctor's gesture. Then suddenly, without warning, the doctor looked up. Quickly, he averted his eyes, but Salas knew he had been recognized. From the pain in the doctor's eyes, Salas also knew that his son had died.

· · ·

Why had the doctor appeared to him? Salas pondered this thought. His years of living among Catholics had taught him something about notions of divine retribution. Maybe as long as Salas had lived the loneliest of lives, the most degraded of existences—someone living as someone else—the doctor had slept in death. But now, had Salas's new hope awoken the doctor? Did he feel the need to remind Salas that despite his great wealth, he would never escape having allowed the death of an innocent child? This was unbelievable and stupid. Salas chastised himself for such thoughts, which came from living long years with sentimental and superstitious Filipinos. More likely, his tension had unhinged him, shaken up the ghost not from his burial place but from some dark corner of Salas's mind. And in a way, hadn't Salas even envied the doctor? Before, he had not admitted it, but the doctor's deep love for his child was something that Salas had never known. Love in his life had always been superseded by duty and the need to survive.

Salas had the taxi drop him a couple of blocks from Plaza Miranda. He held a briefcase in his left hand, which contained the key to the safe deposit box and a piece of paper with the box's location. All had been carefully arranged. Salas heard a singing in his ears that he hadn't heard since the old days when, on the deck of a beautiful ship, he'd marked the time between heartbeats hoping the torpedo would miss, that the plane would be plucked from the sky. Now he was merely crossing a street. Salas smiled. He had always thought that singing was his concern for his men. Now he realized it was concern for himself. He took a seat on the park bench indicated in his instructions and began to wait. The figure agreed upon was five million pesos, which was but a fraction of the worth of the maps. Salas had agreed because the gold had become useless to him.

More and more he had been thinking of Señor Ocampo and his plantation on Negros. That was the life that Salas would now pursue. He would become a gentleman with land, serfs, and position. This briefcase that held the location of the maps was the last vestige of his Japanese identity. By ridding himself of it, he would be washed clean, truly born anew. He was older, but not old. Maybe he would even find a pleasant young woman to pass the time with. He pictured himself on a broad veranda with a clear view to the sea, the palm trees bowing gently in his direction. He sat at a table playing cards with this woman, who had her hair pulled up in a tidy bun. Maybe there would even be a child. Why not? A little round-faced boy with a perfect shelf of bangs falling right above his brow. Kamichi Ayao, once the naval commander, would now be Carlos Salas, the gentleman plantation owner.

Plaza Miranda was a large, tidy field of trim grass, worn to mud in places, and rimmed with trees. A stage was set at the southern end. An arc of high-backed wooden chairs awaited the invited guests. A crowd had already begun to gather around the stage—students mostly, it seemed, earnest in bell-bottom pants. Salas found them amusing, then realized that at that age, he had been in charge of a thousand men. He sighted a man across the park standing by a tree in studied nonchalance. He was wearing a jacket, although it was very hot. One of the president's thugs, thought Salas. He looked around, wondering which of the liberal hopefuls was scheduled for execution. No one was on the stage except for a youthful man in jeans, who gave the microphone a few silent taps, then shrugged his shoulders to an invisible technician. Salas was halfheartedly searching for the technician when Balmaceda appeared almost magically by his side.

The years had not been kind to Balmaceda. He had never been handsome and now—at this proximity—Salas saw that he was yellowed and sick. Balmaceda gave Salas an almost imperceptible nod and the two men shook hands. Balmaceda sat down next to Salas. He rested a briefcase by the bench, which would be switched with Salas's briefcase.

"Would you like to check the contents of my briefcase?" Salas said.

Balmaceda shook his head. He was fretting. Salas caught him looking at the man standing across the park. The man had his hand inside his jacket.

"Ayao, leave," Balmaceda whispered. "You definitely will not leave with the money, but if you're quick, you might leave with your life."

Salas looked down at his shoes. "My name is Carlos Salas."

Balmaceda looked over at his countryman in disbelief. He nodded again, so slight a motion that only one who knew him could read it as an intended gesture. Balmaceda got up, taking Salas's briefcase with him. He did not seem to want to leave. In his eyes, Salas saw the years of loneliness and confusion that separated this meeting from their last. "You have found men to give you orders," Salas ventured, half smiling. He actually meant it as a joke. Balmaceda took the insult silently, but presented his back to Salas. He left with small hurried steps.

Salas inched off the bench, but he was too tired to get up. Then he caught sight of a yellow balloon floating just above the heads of the crowd. Someone had tied the balloon firmly to the wrist of a little boy, whose large black eyes were fixed on it. The balloon bounced spiritedly, tugging at the string, a prisoner of the boy's slender wrist. At this moment, the balloon rivaled the moon and the stars and all the orbs spinning and spitting in the deep blue folds of night. It captivated him as he had not been captivated in a very long time. Then the little boy was staring at him; his free arm was raised to point at Salas and his small mouth was open in a gesture of wonder. Salas saw the father grab the boy by the shoulders and begin to drag him away.

Salas wanted to protest, but he did not know why. He was feeling queer and the sound had drained from the landscape in a way that awed and terrified him. Something was wrong. Salas felt a throbbing pain in his abdomen, a pain he had not felt in years.

Could this be his appendix? But his appendix was gone. This was merely the ghost of it. He patted his stomach and his hands came up covered in blood. The man in the jacket was standing a mere twenty feet away. Salas had been shot. Soon he would be dead and there was nothing he could do about it.

The blood poured out of his side and onto the packed mud around the bench. I am dying, he thought to himself. I am dying my second death. He looked at the awed faces of the crowd and raised his bloodied hands to them. "My name is Carlos Salas," he whispered. But bullets had begun sputtering by the stage and then there was the explosion of grenades. The president's thugs had started a massacre. The protesters were scattering to the far edges of the plaza, running from the rain of bullets. They did not care about rubies or gold. They did not care about the man dying by the park bench. And all around were parents gathering their children in protective arms, finding places to keep them safe.

Intramuros

1. The City

Manila suffered during the war. How many times have I heard this? There are tales of the city weeping in the dead quiet that followed MacArthur's triumphant entry and of her shame at the rubble that greeted him. She wept in pain as bombs blasted away the monuments that marked her time as mistress to the Spaniards and destroyed the infant democracy, a gift from when she bedded the Americans. She mourned for the loss of Chinese and Indian baubles, and for the surrender to the Japanese—her Malay features disfigured by a history of rape and failure. Why would she suffer this degradation?

The image of Manila fleeing down the southern tip of the island of Luzon comes to mind. She bears great stone churches perched on her shoulders, universities in her arms, commerce belted about her waist, and a host of barrios tangled in the hem of her skirt. In pursuit are a plague of tanks and sword-wielding conquerors of the Co-Prosperity Sphere. I picture an *indigena* Lady Liberty warily dipping her toe into the South China Sea.

A city does not suffer. A city knows no pain, nor can it shrink from it. She merely waits for someone to liberate her, and if the liberation is successful, the war recedes into the pages of history.

I shall return Manila to her rightful place at the mouth of a great bay. She curls around it with an arm flung to the east. Her legs snuggle the southern coastline, her sorrowful gaze aimed toward Bataan and Corregidor—if a city could gaze, which it can't any more than it can suffer. Walls are rebuilt, buildings constructed, people reenter the city carting the memories back, much as in the previous year they carted off the dead.

2. Intramuros

The Japanese did not march into Manila. They came quietly— more like the Chinese merchants than the Spanish soldiers. Intramuros—which was a neighborhood bound by stone walls, the legacy of the Spaniards—did not have a history of being hostile to outsiders. My family was of mixed blood; they ate the Chinese moon cakes and blasted firecrackers, learned Spanish, harvested rice in the provinces, and remembered all the pagan superstitions. They believed that the Jesuits were second only to Christ himself and were hospitable to the Japanese merchants who set up their bodegas in the Walled City during the twenties, side by side with the churches, mumbling their rolled l's at the brown-robed friars who purchased soap and bags of sweets there. The old city, with its rat-infested canals and crumbling monuments, was such a mess of humanity that it would have been hard to single out the Japanese. They crept in like everything else and were patient and persistent, just like the succulent vines slowly tearing at the wall itself.

3. My Grandmother

There's a story about my grandmother refusing to leave Intramuros. Most of her children had already been shipped off to Nueva Ecija, where the rice fields were. The Japanese had already occupied Manila, but she didn't want to leave her house. She would stand in her kitchen looking at all the pots and pans, thinking, I don't want Mr. Matsushita getting his hands on these. This is the Mr. Matsushita who probably sold her all the pots in the first place and one fine morning appeared on the doorstep of his shop in full military regalia. Long live the emperor and all of that. I wouldn't want him to get his hands on my pots either. One day a Japanese soldier who was not much taller than my grandmother (and she was four foot eleven) informed her that the house was needed by the emperor. My grandmother didn't much like the idea of her house being a collaborator, but the emperor's representatives insisted that it was not her choice, nor the house's.

I picture her with one hand fixed firmly to the doorknob of the kitchen door (hand carved in the likeness of Saint Joseph's face) and the other wrapped tightly around the wrist of her smiling baby, who can't tell the difference between visitors and invaders.

My grandfather, a sweet, irresponsible doctor who spoiled my mother to the point that she is still hard to live with, was standing knee deep in water in Fort Santiago with other members of the Philippine elite and his fourteen-year-old son. The Japanese had informed the doctor that he could not leave in much the same tone as they'd informed my grandmother that she could not stay. She and the baby, Elena, moved into the church, ate leaves, and occasionally ventured over to the American POW camp, where her father-in-law, a Texan left over from the Spanish American War, would pass her handfuls of rice through the bars.

4. Granddaddy

Granddaddy would not leave the Philippines. He'd left Texas at sixteen and never returned. The story is that he was riding his horse to buy a loaf of bread—something I'd like to believe, but it has the stamp of Filipino romanticism of the Wild West all over it—and never came back. Next he was in Houston. Next he was cooking huge vats of beans on a naval vessel bound for Manila. Then there was something about a railroad that has since mysteriously disappeared. Then he married, had a son, never left. He didn't want Mr. Matsushita to get anything either. I'm not sure when Granddaddy switched residences, but I imagine the Japanese took him first. Finding him must have been a happy surprise for the sons of the Rising Sun: the enemy, drunk and old, wandering around in his house yelling obscenities. They stripped him naked, poked at him with their rifle butts, and had a grand old time.

Granddaddy ended up with the Americans in Santo Tomas, where his son had received his medical degree in the twenties. Granddaddy would joke about it—son class of '25, father class of '45. Things were bad then. In fact, the only up side of internment seemed to be that you met famous men like General Wainwright, a cavalry man with a heavy limp, whom MacArthur had left to hold the fort. Granddaddy had some questions for the general— for example, "Is MacArthur returning?"—but the fall of Bataan seemed to have left Wainwright with little to say.

Granddaddy would save his food and pass it through the bars to his daughter-in-law and granddaughter. He wrapped it in banana leaves. They ate the food. They ate the banana leaves. He would look at little barefoot Elena in disbelief—an angel shot out of the sky and stuck in hell. He would say, "Any news on Richard?" And my grandmother, with her hard, Spanish mouth and sad eyes, would simply shake her head. Granddaddy would watch them leave as they made their way back to the church. She was a brave woman, he thought, with a faith he envied in a God he didn't understand. "Elena and I are safe," she said. "We're sleeping under the altar."

5. Uncle John

One day, an American soldier named John Hachey was wandering through the old city carrying some important piece of paper, and a little boy ran up to him and begged him not to bomb the church because it was full of civilians. John Hachey ran through the streets like he'd never run before, his heart pounding and tears streaming down his face, and he reached the man with the maps and the authority and told him, "Don't bomb the church!" Who would believe that John Hachey—with his southern accent and thinning blond hair that stood up like a wheat field—would return to Maryland and have a daughter named Mary, and that this woman would marry my Uncle Jappy?

6. Uncle Jappy

My Uncle Jappy survived the war, got a degree in medicine (Santo Tomas '56), moved to the U.S., and began introducing himself as "Carlos." I knew him as Uncle Jappy. The more Spanish-influenced in the family called him Tito 'appy. He was not Japanese, nor was he a collaborator, being a mere five years of age when the war started and hardly a man when it finished. His only guilt was in his genes, which expressed the Chinese blood of my family to a startling degree—he could have passed, perhaps, for Japanese. I cannot explain why the family thought it was a joke to call him Jappy during the war, and even more difficult to explain why they used that appellation with all the love and affection implied by nicknames when the war was over. We called him Jappy until the day he died, which was long after his father and brother had left this earth, escorted into the afterlife by the Japanese.

7. Lolo Richard and Fernando

My grandfather and Fernando, my uncle, lived out their lives in Fort Santiago. Who knows what happened? The records are murky. In fact, we only knew that they were in there because someone saw them. How could anyone see them? So many collaborators in those days of hopelessness. Our city, their war. Survival is easy to justify. My Aunt Elena was then two. She'd made it out to the province where the rest of her siblings were crashing around, wondering when they'd have to go back to school. The story goes something like this: Everyone was in the dining room eating and Elena decided that she needed to pee, although her mother did not have time to attend to her. She got left in the bathroom for quite a while. When my grandmother finally got around to getting her cleaned up, Elena informed her that a man had come to visit her. He just stood there smiling and Elena was not afraid, even though she didn't know who he was. He was wearing khaki pants and a jacket made out of similar stuff. He looked like her brother Jorge, only older, a lot older. He had just kind of disappeared and not through the doorway. That's how my family found out that my grandfather, Lolo Richard, was dead. There is no way of knowing how much time he and his son were incarcerated.

I imagine my grandfather with his arm around his son, holding him close, while young Fernando's heavy eyes looked to him for an answer. "The general said he was coming back" is all that he can say. He wonders if his wife is all right, whether her obstinacy has worked for or against her. He wonders if his father is still alive and prays that the other six children have made it out to the province.

8. *Uncle Lou*

Uncle Lou and Uncle Jorge escaped Manila in a truckful of Japanese soldiers headed for Cabanatuan. At first they were confused by the generosity, but after a soldier insisted that they were to stand at the back of the truck and stay visible, they saw that they had earned the ride. Two mestizo teenagers were more than a good-luck charm against guerrilla attacks and American snipers. Cabanatuan was where the Americans who weren't at Santo Tomas were imprisoned. Gapan, the town where the family kept the provincial home, was less than ten miles away.

My Uncle Lou worships MacArthur. My Uncle Lou thinks he's a hero. Uncle Lou left the Philippines for the land of MacArthur shortly after the war. Granddaddy took him on a ship away from his country, just as he'd taken him from my grandparents' house when he was a baby, determined to make him as American as he had once been. Granddaddy returned to Manila. Uncle Lou never did. He joined the all-new American air force. He married his blond, blue-eyed sweetheart. He joined the John Birch Society. He ran for congressman on the Libertarian ticket. He's so American that I—who am half American—cannot comprehend him. "MacArthur," says Uncle Lou, "defines glory." As far as I'm concerned, "glory" is "gory" with an *l*.

MacArthur's at the battle of Bataan facing fully armed Japanese troops, gets all the Filipinos together—most of whom are farmers and don't even have shoes—arms them with sticks, tells them to go into battle and then gets mad when they break rank. Some didn't break rank and that was a far greater bungle. Bravery and stupidity are not the same thing. I have another theory—Americans pronounce "Bah-tah-ahn" as "B'tan," which sounds completely different. I wouldn't be surprised if all the Filipinos got confused and went somewhere else.

9. Tio Jack

If they did, they were lucky. My great-uncle Tio Jack (Joaquim was his real name) was in the wrong place at the wrong time and soon found himself being marched north with a bunch of American GIs. This stroll through the countryside is now known as the Bataan Death March. I'll bet they were cursing MacArthur, imagining the Aussie steaks and fried eggs he had for breakfast every morning. Survival was improbable. A man stooping to sip water from a dirty puddle usually found himself face down in it and on his way to the afterlife. The only choices that presented themselves seemed to be modes of death: shot in the head, dehydration, decapitation, or starvation—you make the call. Dizzied with sickness and exhaustion the prisoners made their way, teetering a hundred miles along the edge of the grave. My Tio Jack somehow managed to sneak away. He lay down hidden in a boat and some villagers, with little thought of their own lives, managed to secrete him away. In later years as Tio Jack—a jovial octogenarian—recounted the tale, he would say, "Others escaped. They learned the Japanese were crazy about staying clean. They threw you know, you know, you know at the guards." In my family, three "you knows" means shit. "So these GIs just pitch it at them, and the Japanese, who would take a grenade in the face for the emperor, go running and screaming. You should have seen it, it was so damn funny." Tio Jack was a great man. He could tell you about the Bataan Death March and make it funny. All of his stories were funny, even though half of them weren't.

10. Benito

A lot of them were about the war, and since he spent the majority of the war with his cousin Benito, a lot of them were about Benito.

Benito, who was not known for his stellar intelligence, is

hanging out in front of this building that has been "liberated" by the Japanese, and the locals are busily "liberating" it of everything of value. Benito lucks out. He gets a bicycle. He stands there, full of pride, watching all the guys leaving with typewriters (no ribbon has been available for the past three years), banker lamps (same thing goes for electricity), and other junk—files, paperweights, rubber stamps. He thinks he might want a rubber stamp, or a dried-out inkwell. Listen, he wasn't too bright. He sees this man standing by him, pleasantly smiling in his direction, a realm of focus that not only contains Benito but also the bicycle. Benito did not question the man's generosity when he offered to watch the bike while Benito went in to get more stuff . . . Somehow, this story is only funny when told by one of my relatives over sixty. Or maybe only people over sixty find it funny, although I found it funny the first thirty times or so I heard it. What I think is odd is that I find myself telling that story, often to people who don't really understand the war or the Philippines or Benito and therefore have a slim chance of finding it amusing. I've decided that there must be some kind of "Benito story gene" that expresses itself randomly yet powerfully throughout my family members. I find myself telling that story to my mother, whom I inherited it from in the first place.

11. Some Family History

She's a war story in herself. All that crap in the basement, drawings from when I was five, every doll, every toy I ever owned — even the ones I never liked. Childhood pictures that I'd like to have, but that she'll never let go. Clothes that haven't fit me since I learned to walk. School uniforms bearing the monograms of religious orders that only have two living members left. Three-pronged adapters to convert currents to levels acceptable only in Australia. Betamax machines acceptable nowhere but Manila. Moth-eaten sweaters that have crossed the Pacific four times, never worn at any port. Shoes with buckles. Shoes without buckles. Shoes that ought to have buckles but lost them twenty years ago when I still wore a children's size eleven. Even the boxes—proud "Mayflower" relics from the first move, when we left Pennsylvania in 1969. Dust and dirt, ghostly smells, odd chills rising when a neglected box is disturbed. Monument upon monument to the past reminding one of nothing more than how very dead the past is. My sister and I discovered recently that we both got insomnia over thinking about all that junk; late at night we think about that mountain of memory and wonder what we'll do when our mother dies. Morbid, maybe, but this happens in families where those absent by untimely deaths play as much of a role in day-to-day existence as the living. Death, among my people, is the inability to disagree.

12. Angela

My mother tells me sometimes of the beautiful dolls that her father bought her—Shirley Temple, the genuine article, with real golden curls; the eyes closed when you laid her down and they hadn't forgotten anything, not even the dimples. Where was Shirley now? Where was my mother's beautiful sharkskin dress with the pleats—very tailored, not like a little girl's dress at all. Her father had bought her a paper doll one day. Over the course of my childhood I received about fifty. And guess what? They're all in the basement. My father has trouble with the basement—he says it's a fire hazard—but I don't really expect him to understand. From what I gather, his experience of war was Ping-Pong parties in his basement and blanketed windows around Boston.

I think of my eight-year-old mother and of that jeepney. It was headed for Nueva Ecija, the provincial home. My grandfather stood with her and Fernando, surveying the interior. There was just one space for a child. He did not see the gravity of his decision. How could he know when he waved my mother on board that he was consigning his beloved son to a fatal companionship? My mother did not want to leave her father and her brother. She did not want to make the journey without them, but my grandfather said, "Angela, you go. If Fernando goes with you, the two of you will fight." They never fought after that. I think, in all sympathy, that people tend to feel the most guilt over things for which they are not responsible. My mother ended up in the country, far from the staccato of the rifles and booming mortar.

13. Her Daughter

When I was little she would tell me of this time when she would wander in the peaceful garden singing a song. It went something like "I can't stop blowing bubbles . . ." and she'd waltz around the bushes, beneath the shade of the tamarind tree with her head full of Gregory Peck and Vivien Leigh. Thinking about that now, watching this scene played out from twenty years ago when I, a big-eyed, black-haired child smiled as she danced, I get an odd chill, as if I'm watching a scene out of *Whatever Happened to Baby Jane?* with an Asian Bette Davis. I hate myself for all the times I've been angry at her.

14. My Lola

For some odd reason, I can't remember my grandmother telling any war stories even though she lived it in the old city shoulder to shoulder with the Japanese. From listening to her, you'd think the war had been one big diet.

"Granddaddy was very, very fat. Then he got very, very skinny."

"General Wainwright was big, then he got skinny. They called him Skinny Wainwright."

"I was not so fat, but I got skinny. Very skinny."

Then she would say, "*Ija*, why are you so skinny?"

15. Uncle Jorge, S.J.

My Uncle Jorge, the Jesuit, visited us in Maine last summer. He stayed for a month. He was on sabbatical. He and my mother regressed to the point that at different times I wanted to say, You cut that crap out, or you'll have hell to pay. If he's bugging you, why don't you just go into the other room? Et cetera. They talked about the different maestras who had shown up in the prewar years to teach them Spanish. They talked about Fernando, who had been an angel his whole life and who, as far as they knew, was doing the same thing, only in a better place. They talked about those Japanese shopkeepers who had slipped them pieces of candy in the thirties, then taken their father in the forties. Then one day, during this odd summer of reminiscence, my mother spun around from the sink, where she was up to her elbows in suds, and said, "Remember the heads?" And my uncle nodded for a few seconds. His eyes crinkled at the edges, and little nervous laughs began escaping his mouth. My mother got hit by the same wave. She squatted down in front of the sink so overcome by laughter that she was silent other than the sharp sound of her inhalations. I walked around them both, going, "What?" After my sixth *what?* went unanswered, I gave up and starting laughing too. I laughed for so long that not only did I feel like I was about to have a heart attack, but I had to go to the bathroom. When I came back, neither of them was laughing; in fact, they both looked a little disturbed. The next morning, over a cup of coffee, my mother informed me that the heads had appeared shortly after the Americans plowed through Manila. They were hanging from every public building, decorating every tree. They were the heads of the Japanese. You learn to laugh, she said. She was not apologetic and I understood.

The Japanese, she told me, would not surrender. To be a prisoner of war meant that you didn't have the courage to die for the emperor, you were less than a dog. The idea was to keep fighting and never to ask why.

16. A Japanese Soldier

This sounds an awful lot like MacArthur. *Dulce et decorum est pro patria mori.* If you were a soldier and not of that opinion, he would help you on your way to glory whether you liked it or not. Such a disposition was good for MacArthur because it gave him insight into the Japanese warrior.

What about the last Japanese soldier? You know the one. He was wandering in the jungles of Mindanao all the way into the sixties, carrying his gun and the love for his emperor, and these two things along with some grubs and wild banana had kept him going. Then they found him and sent him home, maybe with a stack of old newspapers—a lot of newspapers. Never mind, he must have had a good deal of reading time in the hospital. That's a myth actually—not the soldier, but the fact that they found him. If they were looking, they would have found many more people. I know that jungle well. Somewhere, behind a clump of bamboo, are Granddaddy and Tio Jack. In a dark cave are my grandmother, my mother, some uncles and aunts. And if they'd bothered to look at all, they would have found me, because we're all in that last stronghold of the Pacific Campaign or the Co-Prosperity Sphere, as much a part of the jungle as that Japanese soldier or a banana plant or a mosquito. And the jungle is a part of my family. The war lives and breathes like a congenital virus manifesting itself when one is weak. Some of us are less susceptible than others.

17. My Tita Meli

I will use my mother's eldest sister as an example. In her mind, people die and that's okay. During the war, lots of people died, which wasn't okay, but they would have died anyway. In addition to that, we're all Catholic, so aren't we supposed to want to die? Don't we envy the dead their proximity to God? Besides, the more of the family who are dead, the more people there are to intercede on our behalf.

I'm not sure what Tita Meli was doing during World War II. If her behavior now is any indication, she was probably dispensing wisdom and making sure everyone had something to eat. She married shortly after the war when she was eighteen years old. The man she married—a mestizo doctor—was forty-three. He built her a house, far from the rubble that had once been Intramuros, with a fountain and a garden and graceful Corinthian pillars. He took her to Spain where she bought the chandeliers that hang in the sala. He commissioned their life-size portraits that hang in the drawing room. She lived with her mother-in-law, Feliza, and Granddaddy, who spent his final years in a sprawling apartment in the basement of Tita Meli's house. Tita Meli and her husband, Tito Jaime, prospered. Or they squandered. It's hard to say, but they never seemed short of anything. They had five children, the youngest of whom died of a kidney ailment in the sixties. Tito Jaime died five years ago. He was in his eighties. His death had nothing to do with the war, but was caused by a stomach cancer, which, true to the nature of stomachs, consumed from within.

Position

In MARCH OF 1521, Magellan sights the islands. At first, his hands clawed around a telescope, he thinks Saipan to be a sleeping monster. Who else would inhabit this liquid hell where no breeze blows? The crew is starving, eating leather straps and sawdust, hunting rats through the dark, rotting carcass of the ship. They have survived fourteen months of hardship and a mutiny; here, on this sheet of glass that Magellan has called "Mar Pacifico," they fear that they will meet their maker, or the devil himself. The crew has wondered at Magellan's defiant health. They call him "Spawn of Satan" and point to his clubfoot as proof. For someone whose progress on land is slow and labored, Magellan has no equal on the water. He lowers his telescope and blinks, then raises the telescope to the horizon again. The pope has divided the earth in two. The East has been given to the Portuguese, the West to the Spaniards, and he, a Portuguese, is sailing in the name of Spain. He will learn that the West never stops, keeps winding round and round, and the earth belongs to whoever is strong enough to take it.

Magellan's ships, the *Trinidad* and the *Victoria*, draw closer to Saipan.

In the distance, Magellan can make out flat white planes — triangles — shifting across the surface of the water. Could this be the sun refracting, coursing to the left, then right, drawing closer then angling quickly away? Could this be his mind, at last succumbing to his strange diet of leather and rat meat? Maybe these shifting sheets are from the past, a pleasant image heralding his death, because these are sails and the darting movements are boats gliding over the glassy surface of the sea. Sails. As a youth he had owned a small skiff. At the edge of the world, has he encountered the past? Has he wound back to 1495, when, as a youth, boats had been a joy and diversion?

The men are loud, spirited. Their joyful shouting is a strange sound. They have been silent for so long. Magellan is not being lured into the past, nor is he hallucinating. They have reached land and the sails belong to the fishing boats of Chamorro natives. Magellan closes his eyes, confident that when he opens them again he will see his sleeping monsters revealed as islands. Soon he will be navigating his way into the shallows, looking for a place to anchor.

Despite the welcome relief of food and water, there is not much to recommend Saipan. Even the Chamorros are supposed to have been stranded there on a canoe trip from Indonesia, their landing an accident of poor navigation, their decision to remain a mystery. Magellan names the islands "Islas de las Velas Latinos" because of the triangular shape of the Chamorro sails. Magellan registers Saipan in history, much as three billion years earlier, the island registered itself on the surface of the Pacific.

In the seventeenth century the islands are renamed the Marianas after an Austrian princess. The native population is all but wiped out by the Spaniards. Beyond this naming and slaying, there is nothing remarkable about the Spanish occupation of Saipan. In 1899, Spain, facing bankruptcy, sells the Marianas to Germany for four and a half million dollars. The Germans are getting a bargain. They see the value of these desolate islands strung across the Pacific, hard pebbles scrubbed by salt waves. Guam. Tinian. And Saipan. Isolated. Ignored. Saipan's very value is that it is nowhere. Saipan interrupts. It is not the Pacific.

There is much use for something that is Not The Pacific.

Saipan is an island of foreign aggressors, warriors wanting something better, a refueling stop on the way to what is worthy of conquering. The Germans show their hand in the Great War and, after years of battering Europe, lose Saipan (a slap on the wrist), and before Saipan can be allocated to some other deserving European, Japan has claimed it. Japan, the gnat, the least worthy member of the League of Nations, is also looking to conquer. The Meiji Diet has its eyes fixed on China. As a result, in the early years of the twentieth century Saipan is outfitted with a sugar refinery and a fishing fleet staffed with Japanese and Korean labor. These two industries support a significant civilian population. Sharp spears of sugar cane bristle on the island's back and the natives are armed with nothing more than the broad blades of industry. The fish bubble up from the depths and are netted. Women bear children. Tidy huts are erected beneath the shade of palms bordering the sandy, swept grid of streets.

In the late thirties, Japan refuses America access to the Marianas. A fortress like none that has ever been known is being constructed. One forward-thinking Japanese writer, Kinoaki Matsuo, writes, "The islands are scattered like stars across the routes of the United States Navy either perpendicularly or horizontally. It will be impossible for the U.S. Fleet to reach her destination." One thousand islands scattered like beads across the Pacific combine to create a fortress calculated to stymie the American fleet. But what is the assumed origin of the U.S. Navy? What is the destination that will lure its shining ships through this net?

What is Japan planning?

On the first of June, 1937, Amelia Earhart and her navigator, Fredrick Noonan, take off from Miami, the first of many departures on their epic journey. Earhart is to be the first woman to circumnavigate the globe, the first aviator to do so at the earth's waist. Their plane is a modified Lockheed Electra 10E. The airplane has recently been rebuilt after a botched landing on Luke Field near Pearl Harbor during her first attempt at the globe. This is an omen. Earhart has now decided to go east rather than west. She feels the need to make the trip, but admits that she hopes it is her last journey. She refers to the circumnavigation as a "stunt." Her husband, the publisher George Palmer Putnam, is priming his great printing machines for the journey's completion and has arranged for his wife to write a series of articles for the *Herald Tribune* to be cabled from her various destinations. Earhart perseveres. She breaks a record: first aviator to fly from the Red Sea to India. She plows on. Rangoon. Bangkok. Singapore. Bandoeng. In Bandoeng, she is forced to her bed as a result of dysentery contracted in India. She lies for days sweating, exhausted. On June 27, Earhart rises from her bed. She slides her feet into her stout moccasins, rakes her hands through her hair. The mirror reveals her as a middle-aged woman in need of a vacation, not the stout-willed aviatrix she has come to rely on. Her jacket weighs heavily on her shoulders.

In Darwin she carefully packs the parachutes to be sent back to the United States. She wryly remarks to Noonan that they will be no use over the Pacific. Noonan agrees. They need more room for fuel. Coordinates of the Pacific Islands are not reliable, nor is the weather, worrisome for Noonan. He has been groping through the skies using celestial navigation. Cloud cover confuses and extra fuel is necessary to right mistakes. Noonan announces this loudly, which amuses Earhart. She knows what the extra fuel is for, what the secondary purpose of their journey is. The Electra screams off the runway bound for Lae, New Guinea.

On Lae, Earhart writes her last article for the *Herald Tribune*. Pictures taken show her to be sickly and tired. These glossy pictures will be bound within *Last Flight*, the rotted pit at the heart of the book. The stage is set for the ill-fated leg of the journey. She has traveled twenty-two thousand miles and has seven thousand left to complete the circumnavigation. Her destination is Howland Island, a speck in the ocean, with an elevation of less than ten feet. The Coast Guard cutter *Itasca* is positioned off Howland Island to act as radio contact. Radio communications in the area are poor and the *Itasca* has been flooded with commercial radio traffic connected with the record-breaking aviatrix. At 00:00 Greenwich Mean Time, the Electra soars upward.

Earhart is cruising northward of her accepted coordinates. She has arranged with American intelligence to swing over Truk, an island on the eastern end of the Caroline chain. Reports submitted to the League of Nations reveal unprecedented supply deliveries to this desolate rock and the American navy is suspicious. What is Japan doing? Earhart plows on into unfriendly territory. She picks up her radio and nervously transmits her coordinates, which are far to the east of her true location. This is to confuse the Japanese, listening in, from knowing her true purpose. Where is she flying in the deepest night? Where does the sea separate from the sky? Where is the comfort of the line of horizon?

Aviator. Wife. Writer. Woman. Does she need also to be a spy? A soldier of intelligence? Earhart is no stranger to war. She has seen its work. She has nursed boys lying on their cots, watched new blood pumped back into thirsting veins, seen the elbows heal into smooth nubs. She has observed the boys in their wheelchairs learning to navigate the hospital corridors, trying to find their way home. Earhart knows that after conflict, there is no true restoration.

At 19:30 the *Itasca* receives a transmission: "KHAQQ calling *Itasca*. We must be on you but cannot see you ... Gas is running low ..."

And then at 20:14: "We are on a line of position 157 degrees–337 degrees—we will repeat this message on 6210 kilocycles, wait listening on 6210 kilocycles—we are running north and south." Which puts the Electra approaching Howland from a northeasterly direction. Lae, New Guinea, lies in the southeast.

This is the last the world will hear from Earhart.

For sixteen days eight U.S. Navy ships and sixty-four aircraft comb 138,000 square miles of the Pacific at a cost of four million dollars. Nothing of the aircraft or of the pilot and navigator is ever found.

Saipan has a new resident.

Pia is ten years old when the American woman appears on the island. Pia thinks that she does not look dangerous, limping, her blunt short hair illumined around the edges by the sun. The woman has no shoes and her feet are long and narrow, not like any feet Pia has ever seen. They are white like polished stone. The woman walks between two soldiers, defeated. Pia hurries to catch up with the woman. She walks a cautious distance away, parallel with the party's advance, whistling at the birds in the trees, her interest suddenly caught by the barking of a dog. But always watching the woman. The woman stops. She squats down and takes deep breaths. Her face is gray, not like a living person's. She says something softly to the guards, then to Pia's surprise, waves her over. Pia cautiously walks across the street.

She is scared of this woman. Why is she here? Why are the soldiers guarding her?

The woman smiles, but she is in pain. Pia approaches, and then she sees the burns, flaking blackened skin, the whole left side of the woman's face puffed with fluid. There are bubbling blisters all down the woman's left arm. Pia thinks that she is two women sewn together up the middle—one wiry and hard like the bark of a tree, the other slippery and scaly like a fish. She is scared. The woman has something in her hand that she is holding out to Pia. She nods her head, offering, offering, but the child is scared. She presents the woman with her round face, baked brown like bread. Her hair hangs heavily at her shoulders. There is something defiant to the set of her mouth.

Can she read? Earhart wonders. Does she work in the fields? Does she have toys or brothers or a dog, like some of these thin animals tied to the stilts of the houses? The ring came easily off her finger—a gift from her husband, but she has no use for rings, or fingers for that matter. In the instant that the plane plunged into the flat blue sea, she admitted her life was over and now does not know how to think of these days that are left. She knows that her wounds are infected. She knows that her dysentery is dissolving her strength. She knows that the tea and unguents that she has been given are inadequate to restore life. She holds the ring out to the child, wisely turning her head to present the half that was not burned in the crash. The child steps forward and then hustles quickly the final steps. She takes the ring—a platinum setting with a perfect pearl, round like the earth—off Earhart's hand, hopping back to a safe distance. The child smiles, looks up at the guards, who are very serious but young and familiar. The child stammers out a few words in Japanese and the soldiers respond, but the child is not satisfied with the answer. Her thick brows come together and finally she says, "*Gracias,*" with the intonation of a question.

The American woman smiles and says, "*De nada.*"

From her final room Earhart can see workers dismantling the remains of the Electra. She sighs heavily. Her days, drifting in and out of consciousness, are spent trying to relay psychic messages through the radio lines. She imagines the radioman on the *Itasca* picking up the signal.

"It's Earhart. These coordinates . . . She's on Saipan. She says the Japanese are geared for war. Truk is plated with armor, fitted with guns. Prepare. Prepare . . ."

And then they lose the signal as Earhart drifts out of range.

On December 7, 1941, the Japanese bomb the American fleet where it bobs innocently in Pearl Harbor. In this action the pride of the American navy is destroyed, the remaining ships mobilized — tempted — through the string of islands. The Japanese army is suddenly everywhere. One by one the nations fall. Indonesia. Malaysia. Singapore. The Philippines. The Co-Prosperity Sphere widens, a stain tingeing the Pacific a brilliant red. Saipan now boasts troops, guns, and battleships bobbing off the coast. The civilians pack their things into rattan bags, boxes, waiting calmly for the ships that will bear them to Japan. But as the war progresses, an element of fear enters the island. The Americans, once thought to be pathetic, harmless, are now a threat. The soldiers, battle hardened and exposed, tell tales of murder, cannibalism, and rape. Mothers hold tightly to their children's wrists, waiting to be delivered from the island, combing the horizon for the transport ship. Here on Saipan they are served up to the enemy. They sharpen bamboo spears. Machetes, once used for harvesting sugar cane, are drawn across whetstones. The song of blade and stone is heard in every house.

On June 15, 1944, American forces begin the scheduled destruction of Saipan. There are 535 ships assembled in the harbor. B-29s divide the skies, dropping bomb after bomb. The sugar refinery bursts in an explosion. Twisted steel and burning beams heat the ground. Cars are blown upward like paper ornaments. The streets are silenced in a massive boom. When the cloud of dust settles, huge craters where once houses stood are revealed. The chaos of finding children, finding husbands and wives, tallying the dead, continues late into the night. Carrying food, children, knives, the peasants move northward. There is a warren of caves carved into the rock. The Japanese army has already established itself here. Let not the mistakes of Peleliu be repeated. Give the American monsters the beach. Make them crawl the slope of rubble and debris, over fallen men — both American and Japanese—to the dark mouths of the caves. Slay them at the threshold of the redoubt.

General Saito patiently waits for reinforcement from the air. A plane can fly from Japan to Saipan and back. It is safe bombing distance. This is why the American victory here will be the end of the war. But the runways of Japan are quiet, the planes funneled elsewhere or stilled at the bottom of the sea. The Japanese pilots who are not already dead are not of the warrior class. They are humanities students from the university, teenagers, scientists, whose flying skills allow them only one final flight. They are the "Divine Wind," which Saito wryly notes will not blow his way anytime soon.

Bushido. Bushido. The code of the warrior. Never be taken prisoner. Never shame the emperor. Saito looks with pride at the civilians camped around him, their hands poised at the base of a spear. The children collect rocks and arrange them in pyramids. They too will fight to the death. All warriors. All of them. His chest is fired with pride for these simple people and their love of the emperor. He sees in their faces the willingness to die. His words of inspiration come not from hope, but from his faith that all these people—soldiers, farmers, fishermen, mothers, sons, and daughters—are willing to die without the stain of shame. He says, "Our battle is not over. Soon, we will all have the glorious honor of dying for our emperor. Let this not be a wasted death. For each of you, kill seven of the enemy. Kill seven."

Why seven? Why this number? Does the mystic count inspire? Saito wonders as he retires to the inner room of his redoubt. He wraps the ceremonial banner around his head and, taking the dagger in both hands, boldly restores his honor even though he knows he has failed the emperor.

In Tokyo, they receive his final message: "We deeply apologize to the emperor that we cannot do better."

· · ·

The man is screaming, but all that McGill can think of is the man's femur protruding from his leg, the tip of the broken bone sharpened and splintered. This bone looks like a shoot pushing through earth, something you would find on the farm, something the fertile Missouri soil would will into being.

I must help this man, thinks McGill. He wishes he could fix the bone, press it back into the man's flesh, set him up and tell him to walk back to the beach. Clearly, this soldier lying on the ground and screaming has not had a good morning. He deserves rest and maybe a stiff drink. McGill kneels by his head. The soldier pulls in breath quickly, McGill shouts in his ear, "I'm going to help you," he says. The man's eyes are wide and crazy. McGill has never seen so much of the whites of someone's eyes before. McGill says, "I'm going to end the war." He relieves the fallen man of his grenades, then scuttles past on his belly. Two men are lying dead in front of him. One is Japanese, his right hand in a death grip around a wooden club. Caveman, thinks McGill. It's funny. He shelters himself behind these two men. He takes a grenade. He remembers the first time he threw a grenade. His sergeant was holding the collar of his shirt and the seat of his pants. Pull the pin and lob it. Keep your eye on the target. Why was the sergeant holding him like that? Should the sergeant be holding him now? McGill lobs the grenade. There is a satisfying blast. Fireworks. McGill moves forward. Why? Did the grenade accomplish something? He doesn't know. He hopes he didn't blow up another marine. Everyone tells him he's good at what he does. He's a good marine. People are proud of him. Why? Maybe because he hasn't had his legs blown up. That would be bad. That would make him a bad marine. He crawls over more bodies. He looks up. There's a child in the middle of the battlefield. Why? Maybe this child is an angel. Are there Japanese angels? The child's face is streaked with tears. The child is holding a rock. Why? The child throws the rock at McGill. The rock falls just short of where he is lying. McGill doesn't know what to do. Does he grab the child and take him back behind the line of fire? That would seem right.

"Come here," he says, waving the child over. Bombs and grenades are exploding all over the place. There is the whistle of missiles, the stutter of guns. The child cannot hear him. "Come here," McGill shouts. The child screams in fear. The child is bawling now. He runs away. McGill gets up on his knees, trying to see where he's gone. There is dust everywhere—a dense cloud. There is smoke. It smells like a barbecue. No child.

And now McGill can hear loudspeakers, Japanese. And something else. More words. Some are Spanish, he knows that. Must be Chamorro. What are they saying? And now English. "There is no shame in surrender. We will not harm you. We will bring you back to Japan. Please do not be afraid." Who will they bring back to Japan? Who are they talking to? McGill remembers the child. How do they know about the little boy? McGill feels better. They will find the boy and take him back to Japan.

McGill is moving on to Marpi Point. Marpi Point, he figures, is about two hundred meters away. He should be there in an hour and a half, if he progresses at a good clip. The bodies slow him down. Some of the Japanese men are not in uniform. Some are not wearing shoes. Is it casual dress for the defense of Saipan? McGill's leg has caught on something. He shakes it a couple of times, but does not manage to free it. He looks over his shoulder. Eye to eye with a Japanese. Casual dress. The man is trying to bite his leg. Funny. McGill hauls his knee up and throws a kick right into the man's teeth. Where is Marpi Point? It can't be that far off.

He hears an American yelling, "No. Don't jump. Don't jump." The loudspeakers are louder here. McGill pops up and sees the point. He knows that just past his line of vision is a cliff, a sheer drop to the Pacific and the rocks below. Civilians are crowded here together. They are surrendering. Maybe Saipan's taken. Maybe McGill can go back to his ship. He needs a shower. His clothes are sticking to him as the blood dries. His hair has caked into clumps. Whose blood? He stands on shuddering knees (he's been crawling a long time) and hustles to a rock, maybe six feet. He leans against it and looks back at the field of bodies he has just traveled. Amazing. No one back home will believe him. A grenade explodes twenty feet to his right and the ground quakes. He inches around to the other side of the rock.

Families. Mothers with children. Fathers. The war is over, thinks McGill. Go home. And they go, not running, but stepping over the edge of the cliff. A mother holds her fat baby and buries her face in the snug skin of the baby's neck. That's nice, thinks McGill. Then she jumps. Over the cliff. But they're all doing that. All jumping. An old man raises his hands in protest. Maybe he knows more, but there's a Jap soldier there with his bayonet — no more bullets. He urges the old man to jump too. And he does. McGill crawls forward on his stomach to where the land begins to drop. There is a shattered stump of palm. McGill hides behind it. Here he can no longer see the people jumping, but he can see the water. There's that yelling again, "Don't jump. Oh God. Please don't jump." And the loudspeakers. Japanese. On the rocks there are bodies. Children float face down in the sea. A baby is crying somewhere, but McGill can't see it. The wailing stops and McGill strains his ears hoping to find that beautiful desperate crying again. On the rock is a woman combing her long black hair. Mermaid. Weird. She slips off the rock into the water. She disappears. More people jump. McGill can't hear them hit the water because he can't hear anymore. Something about that baby. He shakes his head. No sound. Just people falling, streaking by, their shadows briefly on the water — a hole — then into the hole the girls and babies fall. And then nothing. The ground is shaking beneath his feet from the pounding mortar. He can feel that shaking. He can feel that.

On July 19, U.S. marines invade Guam and on July 24 invade Tinian. The American capture of the Marianas is completed on

August 8, 1944. And what of the Marianas? What now? Tinian is the stage for the end of the war.

The date is August 6, 1945. Colonel Tibbets is the pilot. The plane is the *Enola Gay*, named after Tibbets's mother. The bomb is Little Boy, nestled deep in her belly. At 2:45 A.M. the B-29 super-fortress roars up the runway. The plane is freed from the earth ascending at a steep rate, climbing higher and higher, flying to that height at which the earth reveals itself to be points, coordinates, gray elevations, and glossy blue depths. From this great height, who can see man? Who can remember what it is to navigate the streets in the early morning, to cook breakfast, to dress one's children? Who can hear the broom sweeping the front doorstep or the woman in the next room brushing her hair? Who can hear the crack of eggs against the side of the pan, the sputter of oil?

On the streets of Hiroshima people are moving. Moving. Moving. Packing their belongings onto handcarts, and the wheels sing out on the streets. They are secreting their most precious belongings away from the bombs. They are listening for the sirens, which howl, then are silenced, then howl again. They are walking their children to the parade ground and then home. They are tearing down houses, plank by plank, to clear fire lanes should the bombing come to peaceful Hiroshima. They are bundling letters of dead husbands, departed sons. They are bundling letters from the Japanese army that say "Akihiro died an honorable death in Singapore," or Guadalcanal or Manchuria or Burma. Mothers are wrapping babies in padded clothing despite the heat, because they must do something to protect their children. Mothers are yelling at their children to stop playing in the street when there is supposed to be an air raid—the biggest yet. What sound reaches the pilots and crew?

Who does not want the war to end? Does Hirohito wish to

spend another spring as prisoner of his generals? Do the generals wish to keep fighting? No. They only want to win. How many more must die? What can be done?

Let us all put down our weapons.

At the count of three, we will all put down our weapons. Everyone is listening. The *Enola Gay* roars over Hiroshima.

"On glasses," says Tibbets.

And the bombardier, Major Ferebree, takes his position in the plexiglass nose of the aircraft. He fixes the Aioi Bridge in his cross-wires and locks his bombsight. Now it is automatic. In fifteen seconds the bomb bay doors will open and the glowing uranium egg—the sun's surface contained in a steel shell—will drop to earth.

At the count of fifteen, we will all put down our weapons. There's nothing left but to count. And we start. But it is already fourteen seconds. No, twelve. We must all put down our weapons. Ten. The bomb bay doors will open. Seven. We must all put down our weapons. It is time to stop. We are all ready to stop. At the count of three, we will all put down our weapons.